A S

Longarm turned to the Indian holding a gun on him and said calmly, "I'd like my side arm back now . . ."

The Indian pulled the trigger. The detonation in such a confined space was deafening. Longarm had been braced for it, and he still winced and covered both ears with his hands, too late. . . .

TABOR EVANS

LONGARM

AND THE RIVER OF DEATH

JOVE BOOKS, NEW YORK

LONGARM AND THE RIVER OF DEATH

A Jove Book / published by arrangement with
the author

PRINTING HISTORY
Jove edition / August 1991

ISBN: 0-515-10649-6

Jove Books are published by The Berkley Publishing Group,
200 Madison Avenue, New York, New York 10016.
The name "JOVE" and the "J" logo
are trademarks belonging to Jove Publications, Inc.

PRINTED IN THE UNITED STATES OF AMERICA

10 9 8 7 6 5 4 3 2 1

Chapter 1

Feathered lances, war bonnets, and such were meant to flutter and flash in harsh prairie sunlight. So they looked sort of shabby and timeworn in the glass cases and musty light of the state museum on Capitol Hill. But as Deputy U.S. Marshal Custis Long, known to friend and foe alike as Longarm, strode through the exhibits, he recognized not a few such items he'd contributed personally in recent memory.

But the tall, tanned one-time army scout in the tobacco-tweed suit and pancaked Stetson wasn't there that afternoon to donate the tubular bundle of buckskin he'd packed all the way from the Federal Building under his left elbow. It was evidence, and no matter how Miss Sandy felt about the way that supper at Romano's had turned out, he needed an expert opinion on this infernal shield cover.

He opened an oaken door forbidden to the general public, and descended into the cooler depths of a Denver cellar in Maytime. Doctor Alexandria Henderson was in her corner workroom, staring pensively down at an earth-stained human skull on the worktable she was seated at. The comely young anthropologist would have looked a good thirty degrees warmer than the Indian remains and artifacts on the shelves all around no matter what color hair she'd had piled atop her fine-boned head. But since in her case it was flaming red, and since she blushed ferociously at the sight of Longarm looming in her doorway, he made it more like forty degrees Fahrenheit between her and the long-gone lady whose skull stared blankly back at her.

Longarm knew the skull was female because of the way the teeth, while still sound, were worn way down from chawing rawhide to soften it for her menfolk. He could see from the bone cuts just above the brow ridges she'd been scalped Cheyenne-style, likely with a stone blade. But he kept such thoughts to himself. For he hadn't come all this way to show off about Indians to an Indian expert. He smiled sheepishly down at the blushing redhead to say, "Howdy, Miss Sandy. I got something sort of interesting to show you."

To which she could only answer, with considerable concern, "Custis Long, if you take that thing out again I swear I'll scream!"

He chuckled fondly and assured her, "That war's over, and you won, Miss Sandy. I said I was sorry and that I surrendered unconditional. I'm here today on officious beeswax. As you know, I often get caught in the cracks betwixt the War Department and the Bureau of Indian Affairs because for some fool reason I get along better with Mister Lo, the Poor Indian than your average Wasichu."

She sniffed and said, "I've little doubt some squaws find your crude courting manners an inspiration indeed. But let's get on with it. That looks like a shield cover you have there."

"It was." She made room for him to unroll it across her table by setting the skull aside. For a gal who could surely leap to conclusions about a man's intentions on a love seat, she took her time staring down at the medicine markings of the parchment-white buckskin spangled with bitty black plus marks, or stars, as they were doubtless intended to be. Anyone could see the Big and Little Dipper, with the Pole Star indicated by a more elaborate Maltese cross. Sandy Henderson finally said, flatly, "Pawnee for certain. Most likely meant for a Winter Person of the Skidi Pawnee. Don't ask me which of the thirteen Skidi bands we're talking about, though."

He said, "I won't. It's enough of a thundering wonder for a Pawnee shield cover to turn up along the Bozeman Trail at

2

this late date. It don't look old enough to be a war trophy left over from Red Cloud's War. But neither I nor the B.I.A. can account for any Pawnee betwixt the Black Hills and Bighorns this side of '68. Terry and Custer had Absaroke or Crow scouting for 'em during the last big fight up yonder. Pawnee just hate Lakota and Cheyenne too hard to make for objective scouting and . . . Be that as it may, can you see this bleached hide the right age for the wilder times along the Bozeman Trail?"

She crimped one edge of the stiff buckskin experimentally as, interested despite herself, she replied, "I don't know. Where's this Bozeman Trail supposed to be? I've heard it mentioned but I fear it's from before my time."

He nodded and said, "The Treaty of '68 closed it down. That was the main reason for Red Cloud's War. By the time both sides agreed to a second round in '76, the trail John Bozeman had blazed betwixt Fort Laramie and the Montana gold fields wasn't half as strategic to either side."

He caught himself about to reach for a smoke, decided lighting a three-for-a-nickel cheroot in the company of a lady who loathed him might be impolite, and continued. "With Mister Lo and the buffalo pretty well erased in them parts, the range has been opened recently to more sedate settlement. They got railroad tracks in to all the important parts of Red Cloud's old hunting grounds. So the old Bozeman Trail's just used locally to get from one settlement to another. Hardly anyone with a lick of sense would be riding its whole length across all that rolling prairie these days. But a series of otherwise disconnected Indian scares have been plotted on the survey maps by both the army and B.I.A., and guess what. They're commencing to form a dotted line catty-corner from Fort Laramie to the north spurs of the Bighorns, the way John Bozeman laid his wagon trace out, in the Shining Times, no matter what the Lakota had to say about his wandering ways."

Sandy repressed a shudder. "I know the country you're talking about at least. Mister Bozeman must have been in a dreadful hurry to get to the Montana gold fields. You say he made it alive through the hard central heart of Sioux country?"

Longarm shrugged and said, "I call the folk of whom we speak Lakota, Dakota, or Nakota, depending on how far west to east they might pronounce themselves. I ain't just being polite. As a lawman I'm paid to be exact and Sioux is too sloppy a term. The Crow, Mandan, Omaha, Osage, and such are Sioux, if you're talking lingo and religious rites."

Sandy sighed. "Please don't teach me my own job, you big oaf. I'm paid to classify the poor dears, and like it or not, the people who got Custer are classified as Sioux until further notice. We were talking about Pawnee shield covers in the heart of Sioux country, remember?"

Longarm grimaced down at the mysterious object spread between them and told her, "Ain't supposed to be Indians of *any* description where a shot-up white man made it to the city limits of Pumpkin Buttes clutching this very creation to his breast. He had a couple of buffalo rounds in his back as well. Must have been a tough old rascal. Anyway, as he lay dying in the dust on the edge of town, he confided he'd been jumped by Siksika, or Blackfoot, a couple of miles out on the range."

"Custis, that's insane!" she told him. "The nearest Blackfoot agency lies a good four hundred miles from the range we're talking about, and even worse, the Blackfoot would have to ride through the big Crow reserve and fair-sized Cheyenne agency along the Tongue River, wouldn't they?"

He nodded. "That's what my boss, Marshal Billy Vail, said right off. I'd say the old-timer made a mistake too if he hadn't been such an old-timer. But you see, the man they jumped was a retired army scout who'd fought Horse Indians on that very range in his time. He made a dying declaration he'd been killed by Blackfoot, and I'd say he'd been in position to know. They hit him in broad day. One of 'em caught up with him in the running gunfight that transpired after the first exchange, and that's when the old-timer ripped this cover off his willow shield and sent him sprawling."

Longarm chuckled at the picture and added, "I'd hate to have been that Indian, back in camp that night. It's considered heap heroic to lay hands on an enemy bare-handed. But you sure look dumb if a shot-up and done-for victim turns the tables on you."

"I know all about counting coup, Custis. Get to how our wounded white man could have told a Blackfoot from an

Eskimo at a time like that! To begin with, his attacker was carrying this medicine from another nation. This thing's Pawnee, not Blackfoot, you silly!"

Longarm nodded. "I'm keeping an open mind until such time as we know for certain. Meanwhile, there's no doubt the poor old army scout was killed by *some* infernal Indians, and I don't see how anyone could mistake a Mohawk-headed Pawnee for a braidy-headed Blackfoot. The man said, dying, he'd brushed with Blackfoot, not Lakota nor Arapaho nor Cheyenne, and in his day, he'd no doubt have brushed with *all* of 'em."

"If they were Indians at all, you mean," she said, frowning down at the Pawnee markings. "Brother Lee and his Mormon raiders used a mishmash of Ute and Shoshone trimmings when they tried to pin the blame for the Mountain Meadows Massacre on Indians, no?"

Longarm nodded. "Me and Billy Vail already considered that. There's some mining and a heap of beef grazing going on up yonder on the Powder River range these days, and I've caught white renegades gussied up in feathers and paint myself more than once. But the point is, they got caught, and even the survivors of the Mountain Meadows affair reported right off that they'd been hit by white boys acting silly. I don't have to tell anyone as scientific as you that most Indians have heads shaped way different from our own. White men look unconvincing as colored minstrels too, no matter how black they smear their faces with burnt cork. There's no way an old army scout could mistake white outlaws for the genuine article in broad day at arm's length, swapping bare-handed blows!"

She nodded, grudgingly, but insisted, "I don't see how he could have been dead certain about their *nation*, though."

Longarm shrugged. "Neither do I. I wasn't there. But I can't see him saying they were Siksika instead of, say, Cheyenne unless he had some reason."

He gazed about her cluttered shelves as if for confirmation as he added, "Don't Siksika wear dark moccasins and admire beadwork sewn in sort of horseshoe shapes all over everything?"

She nodded knowingly. "Their moccasins are mostly what we'd describe as dark blue. But you see, the Sioux word *sapa* can mean either black or blue, so—"

"I know how the Paha Sapa got translated as Black Hills no matter how Blue Ridgey they look," he told her. "The old-timer must have noticed some Siksika dress details as they were chasing him back to town."

"Like this Pawnee shield cover?" she asked him archly.

To which he replied with a shrug, "Captured war trophies are good medicine too. Old Woman Owl is confused by arrows or bullets aimed by the army at U.S. Issue, say, or the medicine of friendlies. But I try not to think too deviously before I cut the trail of any rascal they send me after. So I'd best keep an open mind till I catch up with the one who was packing this Pawnee medicine the day a white man took it away from him so desperately. I wanted to make certain it was Pawnee because Siksika and Pawnee have fought so seldom that we might just be able to use that. Old Billy Vail's a caution when it comes to trailing through old government files. Meanwhile, I'd best get on up to Pumpkin Buttes and circle out from there."

As he started to roll up the white buckskin between them Sandy asked, uncertainly, "Don't you mean Fort Laramie? How many troopers do you mean to have backing you when and if you catch up with the hostiles, Custis?"

He smiled blankly across the table at her and replied, "Troopers? This early in the game? You just heard me say the B.I.A. likes me to work sort of delicate, alone. The army's fine when you really need serious fighting. But some officers can be real pests when they smell the chance to win some ribbons for their dress-blue blouses."

He finished rolling the shield cover, ticked his hat brim to her with his free hand, and said, "It's been nice talking to you again, Miss Sandy. But I've a heap of chores to tend to before I catch the night train up to Wyoming Territory, so . . ."

"You can't mean alone!" she almost wailed. "I get to see photographs. Photographs the general public never gets to see, lest they see how wild the Indians really are! The Blackfoot have always been noted for their cruelty, Custis. The Cheyenne are bad enough, but should you fall into the hands of *Blackfoot* . . ."

"I wasn't planning on being taken alive by *any* Indians." He tried to soothe her. "I told you I get along all right with most of 'em, and some Siksika in particular owe me. I caught up with a Wendigo who'd been haunting 'em a spell back, and for the record, they ain't as mean to prisoners as some Horse Indians. Siksika hardly ever *take* prisoners, once they get to dancing about excited in them blue slippers."

Sandy rose as if to walk him out to the stairwell. Then she clutched his sleeves and said, "Wait. I don't want you to go."

He sighed. "I can think of places I'd rather be than the High Plains in early green-up with the bugs and meltwaters rising sort of unexpectedly and Lord knows how many fool Indians up to what. But as I told you that evening on your sofa, Miss Sandy, I got to go where they send me, with little thought for the future and no strings attached."

She shoved the nearby door shut with a high-button shoe as she moved even closer, murmuring, "I know what you said that night as you held me in your arms all aflutter. Do you remember what I said to you?"

"Yep. You said no. I told you I'd stop if you really wanted me to. So you told me you could never go all the way with a tumbleweed you couldn't count on from one evening to the next, and I thought we'd agreed we could still be friends when last we parted, sort of wistfully."

She thrust her body, friendly indeed, against the front of his tweeds, making him wonder what she might have on under that canvas lab smock as she husked, "You idiot, did you really think I wanted you to stop?"

He thrust back, experimentally, and replied, "No man's ever certain about a lady's exact meaning, bless all you undecided little things. But I've arrested many a man who took a no for a yes. So it's better to be safe than sorry when you're wrestling on a sofa with somebody way smaller."

She blushed pretty as a rose and looked away as she murmured she'd noticed how strong he was. "You'll never know how close you came to . . . You know, don't you?"

He knew that right now *she* knew he was suffering a raging erection, if she had any feelings at all down there where she was grinding so swell against him. So he said, "I knew, and I know, and this is getting to be cruelty to animals, Miss Sandy. You said that night it was time for me to stop or make certain

7

promises I'm in no position to make. So what are we doing in this ridiculous position, unless you've sort of changed your mind?"

She threw both arms around his neck and stood on tiptoe to kiss him flush on the mouth French-style. So being only human, Longarm tossed the Pawnee shield cover back on the table and grabbed her back, with her shapely derriere braced against a pine shelf cluttered up with Indian baskets. Once he had a few strategic buttons unfastened, it developed she was wearing only a silk chemise under her smock. As they came up for air she gasped, "Good heavens! You've got your naughty hand on my naughty-naughty again, you naughty boy!"

He got both fingers in the way he knew she liked before he growled, "I can still stop, if you really want me to. But this time, if you let me go as far as last time . . ."

"I want you to go further," she pleaded, raising one high-button shoe to hook its heel against the edge of the table behind his left hip as she giggled and added, "Good heavens, is that a gun under your coattails, darling?"

He said it sure was, unbuckled the rig, and let his .44-40 fall anywhere it had a mind to as he got his old organ-grinder out and thrust it up into her warm wet welcome before she could get as silly about it as she had that last time. She gasped, "Oh, no, it's too big!" even as she raised her other leg to welcome him even more, bouncing her buttocks on the pine shelf as he responded in kind.

But once they'd climaxed that mighty awkward way, she suggested they'd do better atop the table with less in the way of clothing on. But when he suggested in turn they'd do even better in bed, at her nearby boardinghouse, Sandy protested, "Good heavens, what sort of a girl do you take me for? I could never go all the way with a man I wasn't even engaged to!"

So they wound up screwing naked atop that Pawnee shield cover, once he'd made certain they were locked in private enough. Being a Victorian himself, Longarm understood how a well-brought-up miss of her social station might not consider it going all the way as long as they weren't in her actual bedroom without a chaperone. But being a practical man as well, he still wished she'd at least go to a damned old hotel with him.

She said she was sorry about the splinters in his knees, and gave herself to him standing up and bending over with her elbows resting on yet another shelf and a row of Indian skulls grinning owl-eyed at him as he humped her dog-style and grinned back.

By the time she said it seemed safe to go upstairs and shut the museum for the night, he felt less insistent about that hotel bed in any case. He had to walk her home before he ran for that night train, of course. Only they somehow wound up in her bedroom after all, and between one damned thing and another, he never did catch that fool train to Wyoming Territory until next morning, after sunrise.

Chapter 2

The unexpected pleasure of Sandy Henderson's overnight company worked out just as well for all concerned. She confided, serving him his breakfast in bed, that she might not be quite as proper as she let on and that there were a couple of naughty things she'd always wanted to know more about, if only as an anthropologist who was paid to study the disgusting habits of less civilized folk.

He told her he'd be proud to try that Pueblo trick with the corncob when and if he made it back alive from the Bozeman Trail. In the meanwhile she was willing to settle for more usual slap-and-tickle in the time they had left.

Taking that extra time gave young Henry, Billy Vail's office clerk, the chance to catch up with Longarm at the Union Depot. Henry found Longarm and his piled-up possibles near the tobacco stand, where he was stocking up on reading matter and fresh cheroots. The candy butchers aboard the northbound flier charged even more outrageously for stale tobacco and out-of-date magazines.

As Henry joined the taller and far tanner deputy he handed over a manila envelope, saying, "Marshal Vail thought you might be able to use some of these messages he just made me retype for you. Having done so, I'm prepared to state I feel you're both making a mountain or an Indian uprising out of a molehill or an old drunk who got bushwhacked on the open range by a person or persons unknown."

As Longarm hunkered down to stuff the dossier and other reading material in one saddle bag of his battered army McClellan, Henry added, "The War Department simply can't recall when or where Pawnee and Blackfoot might have had the chance to exchange war trophies. There's some difference of opinion as to whether Sitting Bull had Blackfoot visitors in his camp along the Little Bighorn that time. Indians who were there say yes, while your old chum, Crow Tears of the Blackfoot tribal police, says that's just malicious gossip."

Longarm rose back to his considerable full height before he replied with a thoughtful frown, "Crow Tears is a good old boy who's never lied to me, so far, and likes to count coup on all the fights he's been in, including some with us. But hell, the B.I.A. tallies his nation at eight to twelve thousand, divided into at least three main clans. Crow Tears is a Piegan Siksika who can't know everything about everybody."

Henry sniffed. "His agency's the only one within five hundred miles of Pumpkin Buttes. But getting back to that Pawnee shield cover you and Marshal Vail seem so interested in, the Pawnee agency reports all its charges present and accounted for, over near the juncture of the Platte and Missouri, so how—"

"We never said that old scout got run over by Pawnee," Longarm said, interrupting. "As an old scout he'd have never mistook Pawnee for Siksika to begin with. The Siksika he took it from must have taken it from some unfortunate Pawnee, way back when the Bozeman Trail was new and the army had Pawnee scouts patrolling it for fun and profit."

Longarm lit one of the new cheroots he'd just purchased before he added in a tone of weary patience, "Plains Indians don't pass down family heirlooms. A dead Siksika takes all his important possession with him. Anything too big or useless to pile on his sky-burial platform with him gets burnt."

Henry looked uncomfortable and asked, "Why are you telling me all this? Am I supposed to care about disgusting Indian customs?"

Longarm blew a derisive puff of tobacco smoke and said, "Indians taught us how to grow beans, corn, potatoes, and tomatoes too. But I'll allow it's sort of uncouth to let a corpse rot away in a sort of bird's nest if you'll agree that Pawnee-made war trophy must have been packed by its original trophy-taker. Like I said, it's Wendigo to wear or use a dead ancestor's shit, and even if it wasn't, there's no Manitou or good spirit in a trophy you never took personally."

Henry nodded. "I see what you mean. But wouldn't Indian agents, or at least the Indian police, have *heard* about any-one bragging along those lines? I know Marshal Vail's been asking. I get to send all the damned wires. What if some dis-gruntled Blackfoot, out for revenge along the Bozeman Trail, doesn't care about counting coup on his recent raiding? What if it's a private grudge fight between our kind and some sullen old warrior who—"

"There ain't no such animal," Longarm declared. "I mean, it's true you can't beat Indians for nursing old hurts and sulking themselves silly. But any Indian capable of seeking revenge in such a Wasichu fashion would be so Wasichu he'd have nothing much to sulk about."

Henry asked, uncertainly, "Wasichu means white man, right?"

Longarm shrugged. "It's a Lakota term translated best as American, dumb as that may sound. Mister Lo ain't as picky about race as we are. He goes more by your nation and such customs as go with it. That's how come the army has Absaroke, Lenape, and Pawnee on its payroll, scouting common enemies. But sticking to your original question, the old fights along the Bozeman Trail were open warfare betwixt Uncle Sam and the Lakota Confederacy and its allies, under a pretty good general known as Mahpiua Luta to his own folk and Red Cloud to us. If Red Cloud's nursing any serious thoughts about a rematch, he ain't said so recently. He's drawing his allotment as usual over to the Wazi Ahanhan or Pine Ridge reserve. Whether he had any Siksika fighting under him or not, he lost his old hunting grounds along the Bozeman fair and square."

Longarm noticed his private conversation with Henry seemed to be attracting dark looks from a sultry brunette who was reading *Frank Leslie's Magazine* free on the far side of the

12

stand. He failed to see why. She didn't look any more Lakota than he did.

In fact she was much softer and prettier, in her trim gray travel duster and silly summer hat of painted straw and bogus bluebirds. But he didn't care whether she admired him or not, having a train to catch and that other gal to get over.

Henry was saying something about cows and cavalry. But meanwhile, a brass bell clanging somewhere outside warned Longarm a locomotive was about to light out soon for somewhere. So he picked up his McClellan, said, "*Adios,* old son," and strode out to the boarding platform where, sure enough, the Wyoming Flier was fixing to light out for Cheyenne and beyond any minute now.

Knowing he'd be getting off before they ever made up any Pullman bunks up forward, Longarm boarded a smoking car near the rear, just ahead of the club car.

First things coming first, he aimed to make certain of his seat, or at least his share of the baggage rack above it, before he wet his fool whistle at any rolling bar. As he toted his awkward load along the narrow aisle through a blue miasma of tobacco smoke, he silently cursed Henry for making him board so late. For most of the infernal seats were already taken. But at last he found more rump room than he really needed near the rear bulkhead. So he heaved the saddle with all its attached possibles up on the baggage rack, and secured the McClellan to the skinny brass tubing with latigo leathers attached with that very purpose in mind. It was early in the day for even a soft beer. So he was fixing to just sit down and light up when that same sultry brunette appeared amid the blue haze to ask him, sort of sulkily, if that seat near the window was taken.

He told her it was now if she'd like to set her pretty self down while he secured her carpetbag on the rack above them for her. She managed a demure smile of thanks. It couldn't have been easy for her. By the time he had her settled, the train had commenced to roll north through the Denver yards about as fast as a coyote might patrol a fence line for hung-up rabbits. As he sat down beside her she asked if he'd mind opening the window for her, since she didn't seem to be strong enough.

He said, "I wouldn't mind. But you would, ma'am, before this old train rolled very far belching soot and fly ash. I know

13

it's all stunk up in here right now. That's why they call it a smoking car. But once we get up to speed, the roof vents will commence to suck all this smoke out."

She said it hardly seemed possible, and added that she failed to see why menfolk smoked such vile weeds in the first place.

He refrained from reaching in his own vest for a cheroot—it wasn't easy—and replied, "Tobacco ain't the oddest weed folk can smoke, bad as it may smell to them as don't. Have you inhaled, deep, in a Mexican cantina or a Frisco opium den? Don't bother answering, ma'am. I tend to ask stupid questions when I ain't awake yet, and I just had me a rough night."

She didn't ask how rough, or with whom. He knew they had plenty of time to swap life stories before this so-called flier flew them even to the next damned stop at forty miles an hour.

As if to prove great minds ran in the same channels, she asked him if he had any idea what time they might make Pumpkin Buttes. He had to grin as he told her, "I can even tell you when and where we got to change trains, ma'am. For that's where I'm headed and it sure must be a small world, unless one of us is following the other. What's the current population of that bitty trail town—say three hundred, counting the wooden Indian in front of the one cigar store?"

He'd already surmised she couldn't have much of a sense of humor. But she looked even more puzzled than he thought she had a right to be as she said she'd never been to Pumpkin Buttes and certainly wasn't following anyone. She said, "I'm a feature writer for the *Baltimore Herald,* working on a series on your notorious Indian Ring, and so as soon as I heard of yet another abuse of Indians up near Pumpkin Buttes—"

"Hold on, ma'am," he interrupted with a crooked smile. "To begin with, it was poor old President Grant, not the current Hayes Administration, that let the Indian Ring shove political patronage beyond all common sense. I know this to be true because I've been arresting crooked Indian agents regularly for Little Big Eyes, as the Indians call Carl Schurz, our Secretary of the Interior. After that, your remarks get even dumber—no offense. Nobody's been abusing Indians along the Bozeman Trail this spring. Indians have been pegging shots at settlers, and even *hitting* some of late."

14

She sniffed and gazed out the grimy window as if she found the passing telegraph poles more admirable as she insisted, "The Sioux have the right to defend their own ancestral hunting grounds, no matter what some may say about them losing them fair and square."

He sighed. "I noticed you eaves dropping earlier. I do that too. But I listen closely and consider what I might be saying before I say something dumb. That old gent killed by Indians at Pumpkin Buttes identified his attackers as Siksika. Even if he was wrong, the Sioux of whom you speak were hunting, on foot, near the headwaters of the Mississippi less than a hundred years ago. So they ain't been riding romantic out West much longer than *we* have. And as for winning or losing land fair and square, that's the name of the game by Mister Lo's own rules. The Lakota rode in with horses and iron they got from us to take all that buffalo country, by force, from less ferocious Indians, likely Salish or Shoshoni speakers—albeit some do say the Arapaho were on the grasslands long before they got the horse."

He couldn't tell whether he was getting through to her or not. She kept staring out at telegraph poles. He shrugged and said, "Never you mind, ma'am. You go on and write your sad stories about Mister Lo and I'll keep my own opinions to myself. I don't know why I try to tell folks from back East about Indians. Mayhaps it's because I like 'em more than romantical writers like Longfellow must."

She turned back to face him, sincerely puzzled, as she demanded, "How can you say that after the way you just dismissed them as if they had no rights at all?"

He shook his head and replied, "It's folks like *you* who'd dismiss a whole human race as if it was something you had a right to make up to suit yourself, ma'am. To say Indians are this, or want that, is to insult 'em as brainless beings with no minds of their own."

She cocked a brow. "Oh? And I suppose you and Secretary Schurz know just what every Indian wants, or ought to have?"

He shook his head soberly. "Not hardly. Little Big Eyes and me have likely heard more Indians beefing than you or Mister Longfellow. Let's put her this way. What would you think of

15

an Indian who decided Italians were better off eating Polish sausage, or that Greeks ought to take up wooden shoes and growing tulip bulbs for fun and profit?"

She laughed despite herself. Before she could make any dumb objection Longarm continued. "There's way more difference betwixt the so-called Indian nations than you'll find betwixt any white folks in the old countries, ma'am. The Lakota and their Cheyenne allies have less in common than, say, Irishmen and Hungarians, whilst a Pawnee has less in common with either than a Hindu with a Swede. We're talking different customs, different lingo, and way different religious notions. For the record, some so-called Indians make better neighbors than your average Christian, whilst others are just plain murderous and proud of it. I'm still working on what brand of Indian killed that old-timer where we both seem to be headed."

That inspired her to identify herself as one Stephanie Chandler of the Maryland Tidewater country. So he introduced himself, and they seemed to be getting along all right until he made the mistake of confiding he'd scouted for the army during the more recent Shoshone rising over in the South Pass country. She said that one had been all "our" fault, too. So he decided it was about time he ambled back to the club car for that beer. He had to invite her, but of course she refused his kind offer and let him off the hook. He knew petty theft was discouraged along this line by the handy telegraph poles alongside the tracks and draconian Western views on property rights. But there was nothing petty about an almost brand-new Winchester .44-40, so as he got to his feet, he reached up to haul his saddle gun out of its boot, explaining, "There ain't nothing else worth stealing as far as my gear goes, ma'am. But I'd glance up at my carpetbag from time to time if I was you and had anything valuable in it. You don't have to worry, much, this side of the flag stop at Brighton. It's when folks mill about, getting on and off, some few reach out sort of sticky-fingered in passing."

She sniffed some more and assured him she was an experienced traveler. He doubted she meant that the way it could be taken. So he left her to her sniffy self and headed back to get that beer.

As he entered the club car with his Winchester cradled casually over one elbow, an earlier drinker holding up the bar

16

with his gut grinned owl-eyed at him and called out, "There goes all the plans of Frank and Jesse as regards this train. Is that thing loaded, Buffalo Bill?"

It was tough to answer an asshole without sounding like an asshole, so Longarm simply walked around the asshole to find his own place at the far end, where he could set the Winchester on its butt plate with its barrel braced in the angle between the bar and back bulkhead. He told the colored barkeep he'd admire anything they might have on draft, with no needle, this early in the day. He'd no sooner been served and sipped his first suds when a wiry galoot dressed like a cross between a cowhand and an undertaker uncoiled from a table seat on the far side to come over and sort of purr, "I'd be with Pinkerton and I'd sure like to know more about you and that rifle gun you're drinking with, friend."

Longarm smiled thinly and replied, "I got a sixgun under this frock coat and a double derringer in a vest pocket too, Pinkie. But before you get your bowels in an uproar, be advised I'm the law, federal. I'm U.S. Deputy Marshal Custis Long, and you must be new on this line. For I ride it often and hardly anybody's ever cared up to now."

The self-proclaimed railroad dick shrugged. "Our noisy friend by the front door is full of it about Frank and Jessie. But have you ever heard tell of the Plimmons brothers?"

Longarm sipped more suds and nodded. "I have. They're said to be part Arapaho and entirely mean. But they're also said to have considerable time to serve at hard, down Canyon City way."

The black-clad railroad dick made a wry face. "The damn fool state let little Dicky out early because he looked sickly. Big Davey Plimmons busted out on his own less'n a month ago. Since you knew who they were you likely know that, when they ain't in prison, the Plimmons boys rob trains sort of monotonous."

Longarm chuckled fondly and replied, "I wish more owlhoot riders had such regular habits. I hadn't heard they were at it again this spring. I'm surprised they're still running loose. We ought to be safe as soon as this train gets past the next county line. Those Plimmons boys don't like to ride far from

17

home. Pulled that last job well inside the Denver city limits, as I recall."

The less optimistic man in black said, "Denver P.D. says they ain't been seen around their usual haunts since Big Davey busted out. But if they don't hit us this side of, oh, say, Fort Lupton, you're likely right about 'em not pestering us today."

Longarm nodded and asked what the Pink might be drinking. The lean and lethal-looking cuss shook his head and said, "Not on duty, just the same. It's been nice talking to you, but I'd best mosey closer to the mail car now. We'll be stopping at Brighton if anyone there wants to flag a ride north."

Longarm didn't argue. He'd just said much the same to that sassy newspaper gal up forward. He sipped some more beer, and then a more familiar face attached to the railroad came back to the club car calling out, "Tickets, gents?"

Longarm got out his complimentary pass as the conductor punched tickets for others along the bar. As their eyes finally met Longarm said, "Howdy, Gus. I don't need no compartment nor even a bunk this trip. As long as you can promise you'll drop me off at Pumpkin Buttes this side of my usual bedtime."

The older man chuckled. "I figured that was your old army saddle hovering above that swell-looking brunette up forward, you sly dog. As for dropping either of you off in Pumpkin Buttes at any damned time, that ain't my worry these days. I get to lay over up to Wendover, where you and that brunette would get to change to the short line in happier times. Ain't no trains running up to Pumpkin Buttes right now. Indian trouble on the Powder River range. Ain't you heard?"

Longarm swore softly and said, "That's how come me and that newspaper gal have to get up yonder. I hadn't heard anything about the Iron Horse being hit by Mister Lo, Gus."

To which the railroad man replied mighty smugly, "That's on account we don't aim to lead the red devils into temptation. There won't be any serious shipping in or out of the Powder River range this side of the fall roundup. Meanwhile, you and that gal might be able to work your way along the main lines as far as, oh, say, Douglas, where I'd get off and hire me some ponies and pack mules if I was less concerned about my scalp.

18

Why don't you wait till the army makes a few sweeps up and down the old Bozeman Trail, Longarm? Things don't sound too safe in them parts right now."

Longarm grimaced. "I ain't paid to hang out where things are too safe. But I'll pass your kind suggestion on to the reporting lady. She don't know much about her chosen subject to begin with, and could write nice things about Mister Lo in Douglas or, hell, Wendover, if I can get her to listen. What time are we supposed to make the North Platte, Gus?"

The conductor glanced out at the rolling prairie they were crossing as if one grassy rise looked that much different from another. "Either side of high noon, depending on flag stops, train robberies, or fool Indians out to scalp a locomotive. Don't worry. You'll have plenty of time to change to the afternoon westbound at Wendover. That'll put you in Douglas well this side of suppertime, and after that Lord only knows *how* you'll get on up to Pumpkin Buttes."

Longarm thought, and recalled a livery outfit in Douglas he'd dealt with in the past. "Makes sense to travel after dark in uncertain country anyways. How come we seem to be slowing down, Gus?"

The conductor glanced out as if to consult with a calico cow atop a passing rise. "Somebody must be fixing to get on at Adam's Crossing. I wish they wouldn't do that. This damned train is supposed to be a flier."

Before Longarm had to come up with an answer to that somebody opened up with a fusillade of rapid fire. Longarm snatched up his Winchester and ran forward.

The train had slowed almost completely by the time Longarm made the platform between the club car and smoker. He spied a figure sprawled in the dust out to one side as the platform steps stopped even with the splintery sun-silvered end of an open-air loading platform. Another figure crouched on the platform behind a freight cart, sideways to Longarm, as he trained his carbine on somebody farther up the line. He had a red bandanna covering most of his face. So figuring he could hardly be guarding railroad property, Longarm threw down with the muzzle of his Winchester and called out, "Drop that Henry and grab some sky, you son of a bitch!"

The cuss dressed so cow and masked so flagrantly let out a startled yelp, and proceeded to swing the muzzle of his own repeater the way Longarm simply didn't want him to. So when Longarm fired from the hip the contrary cuss let go of his Henry to land flat on his rump and do a sort of comical backward somersault across the weathered planking.

Then, as he tried to rise, well clear of the cart he'd been using for cover, another bullet hit his right cheekbone and tore half his face off. So Longarm shot him again to put him out of his misery as he writhed on the sun-baked planks, screaming like a virgin getting raped with a busted bottle while that one eyeball whipped all about on the end of its bloody stalk.

Then things got sort of quiet. As Longarm peered gingerly out from between the cars, he spied that black-clad Pink striding his way down the platform, reloading his own Schofield .45 as he came.

By this time Gus, the conductor, had joined Longarm on the platform. Longarm growled, "Don't let the engine crew start up before we get a handle on this odd situation." Then he dropped down off the steps, his own gun muzzle held politely, to call out, "Nice shooting. But how did you know, pard?"

The railroad dick pointed at the one they'd sort of spread across the platform and replied in a mighty disgusted tone, "Have you ever seen an honest citizen flag a passenger train down with a bright red bandanna wrapped around his fool face?"

Longarm glanced back down the track at the other fresh corpse. "Yep, that does seem to be a bandanna in the nearby grass. Was the other one waving it or wearing it when you shot him?"

The black-clad Pink put his .45 back in its low-slung holster as he answered, wearily, "Both. He was waving a red one and wearing that blue one higher than it is now. I suspect we just put an end to the notorious but not-too-bright Plimmons boys, Longarm."

To which the federal man on a more important mission could only reply, "You mean *you* did, Pinkie. I ain't asking you. I'm telling you. I ain't got time to mess around with coroners' hearings here, and if it's any consolation to you, there's probably bounty money posted on one or both of the poor dumb bastards. So it's all your own to claim and cherish if you'd like to just forget that one round I might or might not have put in this one poor simp."

The Pinkerton gun grinned craftily and said, "I counted two, including that last coup de grace. But who am I to stand in the way of a federal law-man in such a hurry?"

So they shook on it and the train rolled on with the railroad dick sort of hovering over the two dead outlaws till somebody from the county could get out there to help tidy up.

Chapter 3

Old Gus had been a mite optimistic about uncertain rail service during an Indian scare. It was pushing sundown by the time Longarm ran out of rail options at Douglas, the seat of Converse County, an easy two days by pack or wagon up the North Platte from old Fort Laramie.

But things might have been worse. He'd managed to lose touch with that sullen newspaper gal and read all the fuzzy reports Henry had retyped for him. So now he figured Douglas was as good a place to start out from as any other town along the Bozeman Trail. For unless Henry had missed something, the mysterious comings and goings of so-far-unexplained Horse Indians seemed confined to less than half of the old military route through the Powder River range.

Neither the newer cattle trails nor rail lines between Fort Laramie and Virginia City, Montana Territory, followed Bozeman's original route too exactly, for opposite reasons. John Bozeman had surveyed his catty-corner wagon trace with heavy freight wagons and army gun limbers in mind, winding the most level way around the more scenic bumps like the Teapot Dome, the Pumpkin Buttes, and such to cross the shallow but quicksandy waters of the High Plains as seldom as possible by trending downstream from many a fork.

Gents trailing cows up into the newly opened shortgrass liked to hit as much water for their stock as they could manage. So the extension of the Goodnight-Loving Trail from Texas crossed the North Platte way west, closer to Casper, and hugged the foothills of the Bighorns to take advantage of the more frequent if less impressive prairie crossings yonder.

The railroad surveyors had just as naturally avoided many a moderate rise or shallow draw John Bozeman and the army had been content to live with. Trains ran best where the curves were seldom and the grades rose and fell too gently for anybody or anything just walking to even notice.

The string of trail towns and military outposts that had sprouted along Bozeman's orginal route were still there, whether still in use or not, but as in the case of old Fort Laramie or Fort Phil Kearney, near the modern trail and mining town of Sheridan, folks now seemed to come and go the newer ways. There simply didn't seem to be much call for a strategic military road with no other side to ride against in these parts.

Until recently, leastways. The only Wasichu killed had been that old scout up near Pumpkin Buttes, a hard two nights or an easy three nights in the saddle to the north. All the other incidents, mostly scary sightings followed by a heap of hard riding, had occurred along a thinly settled hundred miles or so centered on that old Fort Paddy Connor had built where the trail crossed the Powder. They'd renamed it Fort Reno, after the officer at Little Bighorn to the north.

Longarm knew they'd named the army post just outside Douglas after the even more unfortunate Captain Fetterman. But he wasn't sure anyone would be there with riding stock for him to commandeer in the name of Uncle Sam. The last time he'd pestered the remount officer at Fort Fetterman, a good spell back, the pompous asshole had tried to outfit him with a wall-eyed man-killer with three white stockings, even though everyone knew you rode a pony with four such hooves or none.

It was getting late to scout up sober officers in any case, and he'd had better luck dealing with the public livery right, there in town. So once he'd supped on roast beef smothered in chili con carne, and washed two slices of mince pie and mousetrap cheese down with plenty of fresh-brewed Arbuckle coffee, he headed for that livery, packing his saddle and possibles on one hip.

The livery was naturally near the railroad stop. It was a good thing he knew just where. For the gloaming light was tricky as the Wyoming sunset painted everything purple on one side and old gold on the other. He'd have doubtless been a goner if a familiar voice not wailed a warning a split second before a shot rang out behind him and sent a buffalo round buzzing through the space his lower spine had just occupied, and still might have occupied had not he thrown his saddle one way and dove the other to wind up flat in the dust in the center of the street on his elbows and gut, sixgun trained back the way he'd just come.

He saw Miss Stephanie Chandler flat on her ass in the same dust with the setting sun behind her to blur everything in her direction, including her. So he had to yell, "Thanks, ma'am. Are you hit?"

She called back, "He was shooting at *you*. Then he knocked me down, the brute! He ran off between those two buildings to our west, I think. Everything happened so fast. I'd just recognized you from across the way, and I was about to call out to you when this dreadful man with a great big gun simply stepped between us and seemed to be drawing a bead on your poor back!"

Longarm rose and strode over to help her to her own feet, saying, "There was no seeming about it, ma'am. When you hear a bullet passing you it's passing way too close!"

Others had naturally been drawn out into the street by that one loud gunshot. So Longarm had his own gun back in its cross-draw holster by the time they were joined by a sad-eyed old gent with a German-silver badge and mustache to match. Longarm was trying to dust the lady's trim derriere off with his battered hat. The town law waited politely till Longarm gave her ass a last good lick and then turned to say, as politely, "We don't know much more than you do. It was a shoot and run with nobody hit on either side, Constable. This lady would be Miss Stephanie Chandler of the *Baltimore Herald,* and I ride for Uncle Sam as U.S. Deputy Custis Long."

The older lawman nodded soberly and said, "We heard you was in town, Longarm. Are you after somebody here in Douglas?"

Longarm smiled thinly. "It seems to be vice versa. Up till a mighty useful suggestion from this little lady I thought I was only passing through."

The town law looked less anxious and replied, "I'm glad. They say you made an awful mess of Cheyenne the time you shot it out with them hired guns across from the city hall. But if you ain't here to arrest anyone from Douglas . . ."

"I don't know where the sneak who just tried to backshoot me belongs," Longarm observed. "I was sent up this way after backshooters dressed more feathersome on painted ponies. This little lady got a look at the one who just disturbed the peace here in town."

They both looked at Stephanie, who licked her lips and murmured, "I don't think he was an Indian. Otherwise he was just a big bad blur. He actually hit me with the stock of that big rifle he was carrying. If I hadn't raised my carpetbag in time . . ."

"We know how you wound up so dusty," Longarm told her, bending to pick up the baggage she'd just mentioned as he gently suggested she try harder to remember more.

But all she could recall about the son of a bitch, in the end, was that he'd been almost as big as Longarm, but dressed more cow, and his black hat, she was almost sure, had been wider-brimmed with a much higher crown.

As Longarm recovered his own saddle and possibles the older lawman said, "That hat sounds Texican. We've been getting a lot of Texas hands up this way since good old Nelson Story druv the first beef up this way from Texas. He only had two dozen riders with him, and Red Cloud still thunk he owned all this swell grass. But them Texas boys were tougher than your average cavalry recruit, so—"

"Let's not go into the opening of the Powder River range," Longarm said wearily. He shifted the saddle to ride his left hip better and continued. "I was on my way to hire me some riding stock. I'm going to need some trail supplies as well, and the stores don't stay open all that late in your fair city, as I recall. So it's been nice talking to you, Constable, but I'd best get it on up the road, hear?"

"What about that mysterious rascal who just pegged a shot at you?" the older lawman called as Longarm turned away.

Not looking back, Longarm replied as loudly, "He's welcome to try again, out on the prairie where he won't have any buildings or women's skirts to duck behind!"

He noticed Stephanie was still tagging along, sort of breathless, when she gasped out, "Oh, I see your plan. You could search about in town for the rascal for days without finding out who he was, unless he took another shot at you. But once we're out on the open range, with no way for him to sneak up on us—"

Without breaking stride, Longarm interrupted her. "There's always a way to sneak up, as Captain Fetterman and many another careless-eyed cuss have discovered too late. But I'll allow I like the odds in open country better if you'll be kind enough to tell me how *we* wound up doing anything out along the Bozeman Trail. I wasn't planning on company—no offense, Miss Stephanie."

To which she replied, as stubbornly, "You *have* to take me with you. They just told me there's no rail or coach service up to Pumpkin Buttes, thanks to you and your Indians."

He laughed incredulously. "How did I wind up in possession of any Indians? I'm not even certain of which nation's on the warpath, if that's what's going on up ahead. Meanwhile, if you think I want anyone riding through Indian country with me sidesaddle . . ."

"I've my own jeans and jodhpur boots in this very bag," she told him, patting it with her free hand. "I brought along a Harrington Richardson .32, double-action, as well. I know how to ride and shoot as well as any man, I'll bet you!"

He smiled wryly down at her. "It's likely just as well I'm not a betting man who'd take money from a woman then. But how well you might handle a mount and such a ferocious weapon ain't the question before the house, ma'am. I got enough on my plate with at least a half-dozen Indians to track and at least one white man tracking me for some fool reason. I like to work alone, hear?"

She insisted, "I have to get up to Pumpkin Buttes. With or without your help I'm riding up there, assuming I don't get lost."

He nodded soberly and said, "You're sure to get lost, and you were about to point out that I owed you, right?"

She looked sincerely puzzled as she replied, "I never said any such thing. It was my simple duty to warn even a brute like you when I saw you were about to be shot in the back. Did you think I did that just to get in good with you?"

Longarm sighed. "Maybe not. But now that you're in good with me, we'd best rustle up the riding stock and trail supplies we'll need to get us both up yonder, Lord willing and we keep our hair."

Chapter 4

As Longarm had expected, business had been slow of late at the livery because of the Indian scare. So he and Stephanie had their pick of a good-sized remuda out back. The Baltimore gal thought one big blue gelding looked "inspired," but Longarm insisted on four well-matched bays about the same length in limb and tooth, knowing they'd be easier to manage on an uncertain trail with an untested fellow traveler.

Having dealt with Longarm in the past, the livery didn't ask for a deposit, and offered a twenty-percent discount because he had his own saddle and offered to pay in advance for two weeks hire. So that tallied to ten and a half bucks at six bits a day.

The livery was naturally able to provide a stock saddle for the gal's shapely rump, and a pack saddle for the supplies they still had to worry about. Longarm's notion was to rotate mounts along the way, so that one pony would always be tagging along with no load at all. One of the hostlers was happy to steer them to a general store a relation ran not far down the way.

Longarm's bedroll, two canteens, and such were already lashed to his McClellan. But of course the fool newspaper gal needed almost a total outfitting from scratch, starting with a more sensible hat. So by the time they'd finished shopping it was late as hell, and the night was moonless as they rode out of Douglas along the river road.

But Stephanie said she'd never in her life seen so many stars, so bright, in such a jet-black sky. He finished lighting his fresh cheroot, glanced back instead of up, and explained, "We're way higher in the sky than you may recall from the Tidewater country. The air's way drier as well as thinner. Some say it was the brighter skies out our way that inspired the Pawnee to new religious notions when they wandered out west from the eastern woodlands. The Pawnee hold every one of them pretty twinkles is a spirit, with the evening star and morning star their ancestors."

"Custis," she protested, "the morning star and evening star are both the same planet, Venus."

He nodded. "Try telling that to a Pawnee. In the beginning their great spirit, Tira-something-or-other, felt lonesome floating about in nothing much. So he created Sun and Moon for company. They got hitched and produced all the other lights up yonder, and that might have been that if Morning Star and Evening Star hadn't produced Corn, First Pawnee, and other important beings. It was the other stars, likely jealous, who gave birth to First Fly, First Sioux, and other less useful objects."

She smiled up at the Milky Way to say she could see how the Pawnee might have come by such notions under such a heavenly sky. Then she asked how come he kept looking back.

He said, "Trying to see if we're being followed. You said that sneak that pegged that rifle shot at me ducked between two buildings. You never said he'd eloped to Niagara Falls."

She repressed a shudder and said, "Good heavens, you're right, and what if there's more than one of them after us?"

He shrugged. "I doubt anyone's after *you*. If they hadn't been more interested in *me* back yonder, I fail to see how we could be having this conversation. But hold the thought, rein in quiet, and just be still a spell."

She reined in with no more argument than the two extra ponies he'd been leading. But he had to hush her with a hiss when she asked how come. After a few moments of silence he shrugged and said, "I'm sorry I shushed you so rudely just now. I thought I was hearing other hooves in the middle distance, and

29

there's nothing within a country mile our own mounts could be bouncing echoes off."

She gasped and whispered, "Oh, Lord, whatever shall we do?"

To which he could only reply, "You can call me Custis, in private. There's nothing much we *can* do, on this public right of way, that'd be all that safe for the general public. We're smack on the old Oregon-and-Other-Points-West Trail."

She demurred. "I thought you said we were following the Bozeman Trail." He replied, "That too. Most everybody follows the North Platte upstream this far, at least, and us law-abiding lawmen ain't allowed to bushwhack night riders who might be headed most anywhere on innocent business."

She pointed out, "No innocent traveler would have any reason to rein in and sort of sulk, back there, just because they heard us stop, would they?"

"It ain't likely," he said. "But it's possible. We might not be the only ones with cautious natures. Most anyone out on any trail this late would have heard the same grim tales of Blackfoot off the reserve. Let's ride on and see if we hear any more echoes."

They did both. His brunette traveling companion softly called out, "They're pacing us, just downstream! I'll bet they're watching that cigar you're still puffing on, you idiot!"

He chuckled and replied as softly, "It's a cheroot, not a cigar, and I don't want 'em closing in too close just yet. I make it two ponies tagging along just outside rifle range. Too early to say if it's two riders or one gunslick leading a pack pony. Either way, the plan is to dog us at a safe distance for now."

He took a drag on his smoke to flare the red tip good before he mused, half to himself, "It works two ways just as well. Someone could be simply headed up towards, say, Casper on innocent beeswax, or a more murdersome someone could be planning to wait till we turn off this more-traveled trail. As I already told you, the Bozeman's hardly used by anyone important lately. Lord knows how long a body or two might rot a few miles north of the river before anyone but the carrion crows and coyotes would notice."

She softly protested, "I don't want to rot whether anyone notices or not, Custis! Wouldn't it make more sense to make a stand here and now, on the beaten path?"

He grimaced. "It might, if I didn't fear those echoes would simply beat it as soon as we seemed to be forting up. Let's see now. We're only a couple of miles from where the old Bozeman wagon ruts fork off this riverside trail and—"

"There's somebody standing by the side of the road ahead!" she suddenly said, reining her pony to a halt as Longarm slowed but kept going. She caught up again as he reined in closer to the mysterious patch of blacker darkness that had caught her worried eye. He thumbed a match head alight as he explained, "Trail sign. Mounted on a cottonwood pole. Some neighborly wagon master noticed how easy it was to bog a wagon wheel along this stretch, and left this warning to swing out from the water a tad."

He shook the match out, but not before he'd noticed the bullet holes some asshole had punched through the neatly lettered wooden placard in passing. He rode a mite closer to reach out and stick his half-smoked cheroot's wet end in a handy bullet hole. Then he softly told the girl, "That ought to hold 'em back a piece for now. I want you to follow my lead slow and soft across the grass. Try not to even creak your pretty behind in that old saddle, and I'll explain what we're trying to pull off as soon as I see whether we've pulled it off or not."

She must have been bursting, but to her credit she tagged along as silently as the pack ponies until Longarm had led his little expedition a couple of furlongs north and then, finding a modest grassy rise under them, reined in and swung around, softly drawing his Winchester from its saddle boot.

Stephanie gasped, "Do you think anyone's coming?"

He rested the Winchester across his thighs, resisting the impulse to lever a noisy round into the chamber as he quietly replied, "If anyone is, I just wasted some good tobacco. I stuck that smoke in that sign to discourage anyone from coming close enough to hear us tiptoe off the trail. If nobody did, I doubt we left enough sign to matter on thick sod at a walk."

One of the pack ponies farted and let fall a half-dozen horse apples. So Longarm smiled thinly and added, "Until just now, at any rate. Innocent parties ought to ease around anyone halted on the riverside trail ahead of 'em. Less innocent parties likely

31

know we were on our way to the regular cutoff upstream."

As if to prove his point they both heard distant but determined hoofbeats, moving from left to right as they stared south at nothing much by starlight. Yet even a Baltimore gal could put what was happening together. So she laughed and said, "Oh, my, I'll bet they were really mad when they finally caught on to your trick with that bitty cigar! Listen to them go, trying to catch up with us!"

He chuckled and said, "Yep. Whether they do or don't, they'll head north along the regular Bozeman, once they come upon it. That gives us the chance to turn some tables, knowing where they figure to pass next instead of vice versa. So we'd best get cracking, hear?"

She heeled her own pony into motion as he took the lead again, and called out, "Where are we going? How can you see any trail across this wide-open space in the dark?"

He repressed a snort of disgust and kept his tone polite as he patiently explained. "There isn't any trail. I just told you John Bozeman's wagon trace parts company from the beaten path from Fort Laramie a good two miles or more to the west. But we ain't freight wagons or army caissons. So this rise barely slowed us enough to notice. Our mounts can see by starlight well enough to keep us from riding into anything important as long as we don't ride too sudden. So let's ride, Powder River and let her buck!"

They did, albeit she kept yelling in concern, if not sheer terror, as Longarm led them cross-country at a jarring but mile-eating trot. He had the stars to navigate by, and meant what he'd said about the night vision of your average pony. But not knowing just how average these ponies were, he resisted the impulse to lope 'em in the dark. He'd had a pony step in a prairie-dog hole in broad-ass daylight in his time, and this was neither the time nor place to take such chances. They came to a steeper rise than usual. Once they'd topped it, Longarm reined in, saying, "The ones we've been riding sound winded. This'd be a good chance for you to take a leak, whilst I'm changing our saddles about."

She gasped in dismay and asked if that was any way to talk to a lady. To which he could only reply, "Ladies leak too. But if you're some sort of angel, forget my crude manners and just don't expect me to stop until I figure we're out ahead of those other ponies, hear?"

So she dismounted and went off somewhere to piss in private while he swapped the saddles about and pissed as discreetly. Traveling with a female you weren't screwing could sure get awkward.

Chapter 5

The almanac Longarm had consulted on the train from Denver had told him to expect a mighty late moonrise that night. The moon still peeked over the horizon earlier than the sun, and after all that peering about by starlight, their eyes found its pale rays one hell of an improvement.

Having already figured about where they had to be, by moonrise, Longarm had tethered the four ponies in a timbered draw to browse on fresh cottonwood shoots as he took Stephanie and his Winchester up atop a grassy rise to their west. He paused to get their bearings. "That faint chalky line across yonder blackboard has to be the Bozeman, and so far, there ain't nobody here but us chickens. It's a far shot, but I can likely spill a pony down there from up here if I have to. There's no cover any closer. So here's where we'd best hunker, ma'am, unless you'd rather stay down yonder with the riding stock."

She told him not to be silly. So he nodded and pointed at the best cover along the crest of the rise, saying, "Be careful about your face as you stare out from behind them vegetable sea urchins, ma'am. The spines are sharp as they look."

She knelt in the grass in her thin jeans and gingerly felt the nearest soapweed tips. "You're right. What is this, some variety of cactus?"

34

He flopped beside her in the buffalo grass, Winchester trained on the trail below as he reclined on his elbows, saying, "Some kind of spitesome lily would be closer, ma'am. They call it yucca down where Spanish is more spoken, and soapweed or bear grass up this way. The Western beef industry was started by Spanish-speakers. But as you work north it gets more gringo."

She reclined on one hip beside him. "I'd rather call it yucca when I write about all this for the *Herald*. What was that about Powder River and letting who buck?"

He smiled, wistfully, and explained. "I reckon I picked that up from an old cowhand called Roping Sally. It started on the Goodnight Trail up from Texas, a few summers back, as they were opening this north range up."

"Never mind who started it," she insisted. "What does it mean?"

He said, "Oh, that's easy. Starting out from Texas or anywhere, the cows are cranky and the ponies would rather buck you off than take you anywhere. So Powder River and let her buck means something like we're heading where we're headed no matter what, see?"

She hesitated. "I think so. I don't see why you people can't talk like everyone else. If that Bozeman Trail down there goes to Powder River, where's that Goodnight Trail you just mentioned?"

He caught himself reaching absently for a smoke, decided not to, and replied. "The cattle trails are over to the west, along the foothills where the grass stays greener longer, and the draws run wet as late as August. John Bozeman wasn't interested in the Powder River or any other river when he blazed that trail down yonder. He was out to avoid as many water crossings as he could on the way to a gold mine through Indian country. Lord willing and we make it, you'll not have to ford betwixt here and Pumpkin Buttes."

She sounded disappointed as she demanded, "How come? I was led to expect Pumpkin Buttes in the heart of the Powder River country."

"It's this side of the actual Powder River crossing," he told her, adding, "The trail town we're talking about enjoys a fine view of Pumpkin Buttes. Nobody with a lick of sense would want to live on top of all that orange rimrock. The monstersome stretch of open range betwixt the Bighorns and the Black Hills is only *drained* by the Powder River and all its infernal tributaries. John Bozeman's genius lay in avoiding as many quicksandy draws as possible to cross the wide but shallow main stream at Fort Connor, Fort Reno, or whatever in thunder they're calling it now. The last I'd heard, most of the old army posts along the Bozeman had been abandoned."

He kept forgetting she was a newspaper gal, paid to be at least as nosey as any lawman. She demanded to know why the army had built a string of military outposts only to abandon them. He growled, "We ain't got time for a history of the Lakota Confederacy, even if it was all that interesting. Suffice it to say, Red Cloud won the first few battles, and guess who won the last ones. With the Indians shot off and the range opened up to beef and homesteading, there's just no point in having a string of army posts along a military road that hardly anybody uses."

She removed the broad-brimmed farmer's hat he'd made her switch to back at that general store, and laid it aside on the buffalo grass as she yawned, stretched graceful as a cat, and said, "I'm just glad we won't be riding as far as I feared. I confess I'm not accustomed to riding as far as I just have astride, and don't you western riders ever bother to sleep at all? It must be well past midnight and—"

"We'll have all day to snore, provided you'll be a sport about taking turns with both red and white rascals out to do Lord knows what to us." He added, "In Indian Country you hide out and sleep by day so's you can ride at night, hear?"

She said, "Pooh, I thought you just said this was cattle country now. Who was Roping Sally and what else were the two of you up to when she wasn't teaching you to let her buck along the Powder River?"

Longarm stared hard at that empty trail down yonder and let his breath half out so his voice wouldn't crack as he soberly replied, "I don't like to tell funny tales about the dead, ma'am. Let's just say Roping Sally was a good old gal who had a cow spread up Montana way, near the Blackfoot agency. The reason they called her Roping Sally went with her chosen occupation. She was good at it. Damned good at it."

Stephanie didn't ask what else the lady in question might have been good at. She asked what had happened to her. So Longarm swallowed hard and murmured, "She was murdered. I got the hired killer that done the deed and then I got the crooked land agent that hired him. So let's not talk about it no more. What happened up yonder couldn't have nothing to do with what's been happening down this way, hear?"

Stephanie kept on. "The Indians who killed that retired army scout were Blackfoot, and you say this other girl was killed up by the Blackfoot agency, Custis?"

Longarm swore under his breath and growled, "Roping Sally wasn't killed by any Siksika, damn it! She was killed by crooks who were out to rob the Indians. The Indians *liked* old Roping Sally, see?"

She said, "I'm trying to, Custis. What are you so upset about? Were you . . . in love with that unfortunate thing?"

He snapped, "Sally was no *thing,* damn it! She was a sweet and loveable human being who could ride better than most men, kiss better than most women, and as to how we might or might not have felt about one another, that son of a bitch pretending to be an evil spirit killed her before we'd known one another long enough to work that out."

He caught himself getting more excited than he liked to let himself, and looked away, muttering, "Jesus H. Christ, can't a man mention one poor gal to another without getting cross-examined about his personal feelings?"

She softly replied, "I suppose it depends on how attractive women find him. Was she prettier than me, Custis?"

He laughed despite himself and truthfully replied, "That'd be like comparing a prairie pasqueflower with eastern violets, Steve. Since you just won't let it alone, the late Roping Sally was bigger, blonder, and built more boyish than yourself. I'm in no position to say which of you might or might not be the better lay."

He'd meant that to jar her and it must have, judging from the odd little noises coming out of her as she leaped to her feet and ran off downslope towards their ponies. He growled, "Women!" and turned his gaze back to that moonlit wagon trace down the other way. He was dying for that smoke, and if they'd cut anyone trailing them off, where in thunder might the one or more sons of bitches be right now?

Trying to place himself in someone else's saddle, Longarm considered how far he could have ridden the long way round, given a clearer path along more level ground but considering someone with a Winchester and a known rep somewhere out ahead in the dark.

He reached a conclusion. "Reckless assholes have come after us in the past. If even one of 'em already knows this range a mite better, they might have risked loping whilst more sensible riders were trotting."

He plucked a grass stem to chew as he considered all options. There was still some taste to the juicy stem this early in the green-up of the north range. The grazing would be prime most of the summer, in every direction all around. You didn't really have to stick to any beaten path across this great rolling sea of grass and frequent water holes. Red Cloud had known what he was up to when he'd tried to keep the Wasichu and his cows out of this country, the poor bastard. So as soon as one studied, it seemed obvious they didn't have to follow the Bozeman Trail to Pumpkin Buttes rut by rut. Knowing where the trail town was, and knowing he'd be operating half blind until he had some help from local riders, he considered the advantages of riding in sort of unexpected from, say, around the far side of those buttes the fool town was named for. That'd surely put a crimp in the plans of anyone either trailing them or already out ahead, lying in wait like this on some other infernal rise.

Of course, there was always another way to look at anything. So when he noticed Stephanie coming back up the slope, as if she might have forgiven him after all, Longarm rolled half over to call out, "I don't think they'll be along down yonder. We might have lost 'em down by the river, or they're being just as cute about heading folks off up the trail. What's that you've dragged up here, Steve?"

She tossed the loose bedding on the grass between them and told him, in a sort of pouty way, "It's getting cold as anything up here, in case you haven't noticed. How long are we liable to be stuck on this old windswept hilltop?"

He said, "I was just about to suggest we forget the fool trail for now and cut around to the north of the Pumpkin Buttes. They occupy a sort of drainage divide betwixt the Dry Fork of the Powder and the Belle Fourche running off towards Devil's Tower, another butte entirely."

She dropped to her knees again on the bedding, asking, "Does that mean I unpacked all these blankets for nothing?"

"We won't want to move on just yet either way. Lord only knows who else might be out here amid all this nothing much, and if we stick to riding by night and laying low the rest of the time, I figure we'll reach the town we're aiming for in two nights with luck. The luck of which I speak calls for offering a lady her choice, Steve. The farther we ride alone, the more likely we are to bump noses with the Indians, who've been hitting along the trail but camping somewhere else. On the other hand, if we follow the trail more directly . . ."

"Let's worry about that when the time comes," She said, lying back on the covers. "If we're going to ride by night and snuggle by day, we've a whole day ahead of us to talk about that, right?"

That inspired him to sit up, propping the Winchester's muzzle in some dry soapweed as he got rid of his own hat, saying, "It sure does, and now that you mention it, we'd be as safe from bugs and other surprises up here in this knee-high nest of cover, as long as we kept our heads close to the ground leastways."

She said, "I wasn't planning on sleeping on my feet, were you?"

He laughed and replied, "Not hardly. But I'd best fetch my own bedding, some water, and our breakfast whilst it's still dark."

As he got to his feet she told him, in that same pouty voice, "I can see what you mean about water and something to nibble on up here. But do you really think you'll need your own bedroll, Custis?"

He laughed and joined her atop her ground cloth and covers to take her in his arms as he soberly replied, "Don't even need the food and water yet. So why waste such a swell prairie moon on chores that can wait?"

She kissed him back as warmly. He really couldn't say whether she kissed as warm as poor old Roping Sally had. It was never exactly the same, bless all their sweet lips. But as he slipped his free hand inside her flannel shirt to see how else she might or might not feel the same, Stephanie

39

gasped and pleaded, "Wait. Not so directly to my forbidden fruit, cowboy."

To which he could only reply, with a sigh, "I didn't know it was forbidden, ma'am. Let's just say no more about it."

But as soon as she saw he really meant it, she grabbed his wrist to guide his hand where he'd only planned on putting it much later as she husked, "Oh, damn, let's just say Powder River and let her buck, if that's the way you Western wild men want to put it!"

So he hauled her jeans off and shucked his own duds so he could put it right where they both wanted him to put things. Albeit she wanted to keep her flannel shirt on against the chill night air, until he'd brought her to climax the first time.

After which she thought it might be more fun under one blanket, naked as a jay, as she did most of the work on top. So with one thing and another, the sky to the east was suddenly pearling rosy, and he had to run some as he got that food and water back up to their love nest on the rise just ahead of sunrise.

By the time they'd eaten cold canned beans, washed down with tomato preserves, the sunlight washing over their naked bodies made her feel like blushing, she said.

He said it made him feel like staring all over, and as he entered her again, by the dawn's early light, she begged him to close his eyes too as he moved it in and out of her. But of course he never did, and they both laughed like mean little kids when he caught her staring down between them too.

Later, sharing a dreamy smoke with him atop the rise, she murmured, "I suppose you want to know how I lost my virginity and got to be such a naughty little goose, right?"

He snuggled her closer, patted her bare shoulder reassuringly, and declared, "I've yet to figure why they call learning something grand about life's pleasures a loss. As to why one feels naughty once one's lost one's ignorance, it feels good to fornicate, as everyone but Queen Victoria and some other stuffy folk could tell you, if only they'd admit it. I read this magazine piece a spell back, explaining how youthful libertines are led astray by penny-dreadful reading and tailor-made smokes. That's what they call a kid who'd rather get laid than sweep out a cellar, a youthful libertine. The gent who wrote

40

the fool piece must not have known what it felt like to come, judging from his prescriptions for purity."

"I was seduced by an older friend of the family when I was seventeen, God bless him," she began.

But he stuck the cheroot in her pretty mouth to shut her up as he told her, "I just said it felt swell to fornicate, and I'll be switched with snakes if I can see why you gals all feel the need to justify such swell feelings by blaming it all on some other son of a bitch! I don't want to hear how you lost your fool cherry, as long as I don't have to worry about it."

She put the cheroot to his lips as she demurely replied, "I just thought you might be curious, dear. I confess that trick with your elbows hooked under my knees was a novelty to me. Did that Sally person teach that to you?"

He got rid of the cheroot and hauled the top tarp up to protect their nude hides from a serious prairie sunburn as he confessed, "We were both experienced riders before we ever rode together. Tricky riding is tougher on a bronc. You get to fall so far when you fail to bounce in unison with your mount."

She told him he bounced just swell, yawned, and added, "Between you and those other beasts spreading my poor thighs so far for so long, I'm having a hard time staying awake."

He patted her bare shoulder and said, "Go ahead and close your pretty eyes then. I'll wake you up around noon and you can keep watch whilst I saw some wood."

She yawned again but asked, "Are you sure we're safe up here?"

He nodded and assured her, "Safer and less bug-bit than we might be down in that draw with the livestock. We're hunkered in soapweed atop the highest crest for miles. As long as one of us remains half awake up here, nobody figures to get anywhere near us without being spotted long before he, she, or it can draw a bead on us."

She stretched like a kitten and rolled her shapely bare back to him. Then she spotted what he'd hoped she might not, against the cobalt blue sky to their north, and propped herself up on one elbow to flatly declare, "I see smoke rising! A whole daisy chain of smoke signals rising higher and higher and—oh, Custis, do you think some Indians could be over that way?"

41

He hauled her back down against him, saying soothingly, "I'd be more surprised to hear a Swede was sending up them signals. Try to keep any sudden moves below the level of the soapweed all around us, Steve. That rise they're on is a good eight or ten miles off and no higher than this one, but why take chances?"

She said, "We have to get dressed and make a run for it."

To which he replied, with another shrug, "How come? We knew there were Indians out this way, and that smoke talk can't be about us."

She brightened and asked, "Can you read those smoke signals, dear?"

He shook his head soberly and replied, "Ain't nobody supposed to. I savvy Horse Indian sign. The hand signals are the same and mean the same no matter what the Indian's own lingo might be. Some say it was invented by the Kiowa or Comanche when they noticed others moving in on 'em with ponies in their Shining Times or golden age. Strangers meeting on the prairie might want to fight or they might want to swap or go hunting together. I've managed to sign my way out of a fight with the little any Wasichu can manage. But smoke talk is meant for private conversations with distant pals. So they change the code as they go along. Steady columns usually mean about the same to one and all, since they're sort of public notices. One column means something's up and all concerned ought to keep their eyes open. Two columns rising side by side mean everything's jake and any pals within miles are welcome to visit. Three columns, like three shots, mean someone's in trouble, red or white, west of, say, the Blue Ridge Mountains of Virginia."

She decided there was one smudge fire burning on that distant rise to the north. Before she could say anything dumb Longarm told her, "I'd hazard someone's using that other rise as a lookout whilst others are patrolling the range all about. So them smoke puffs are telling riders down off that rise about something that's been spotted from atop the rise."

She repressed a shudder and demanded, "Who could it be, if you're sure it's not us?"

He said, "Somebody else, of course. Nobody's passed us from the south since we've been up here. Somebody could

42

be headed south along that trail down yonder. If they make it, we'll spot them long before they can hope to spot us. If they don't, we won't. Meanwhile, try and get some sleep. I'll be here, watching over you."

She sighed, and reached behind her bare rump to pat him in a sort of sassy way. It wasn't long before she was, in fact, asleep.

Longarm envied her. His body was tired enough, but his mind was wide awake and likely to stay that way. For he wasn't half as sure as he'd let on that nobody was discussing his sex life and present whereabouts in smoke talk. Those fool Indians over yonder were surely having a long conversation about *somebody* right now.

Chapter 6

The balmy spring day was just meant for lazing away in the company of a beautiful bare brunette, or would have been had Longarm felt more certain of their continued existence. Since he didn't, they managed fitful turns asleep, and enjoyed trail grub and each other in each other's company until, at last, the damned old sun went down and they felt it safe to get up and get dressed.

He naturally left Stephanie forted up on the rise as he scouted their riding stock, down in the wooded draw, with his Winchester at port arms and his asshole puckered more than he'd thought it might be until he found all four ponies alive and well and, above all, *alone* where they'd been tethered amid cottonwood and peach willow spiced with a few fresh shoots of wild cherry. Wild cherry seldom got thick enough to matter where either cows or ponies could get at it. Buffalo had been more considerate of wild cherry in the Shining Times, accounting for all sorts of Cherry Hills and Cherry Creeks in parts of the West where a cherry of any sort was considered a rare find.

Longarm watered the stock and refilled the canteens up the clear seep from where the horses had been tethered to browse and fertilize the draw all day. Then he fetched Stephanie

44

and her rolled-up bedding down off the rise and helped her mount up.

She was a good enough sport about it till she noticed the way they seemed to be heading. When she bitched that she liked her hair just the way it was, he said soothingly, "That smoke talk faded away the other side of noon, honey."

She asked what made him so sure the Indians had faded away as well. He shrugged. "We got to ride north, whether east or west of that rise and the Pumpkin Buttes beyond. I don't much cotton to our following the Bozeman Trail directly. For that's what I'd be expecting foolhardly folks to do if I was wearing feathers and paint right now."

"How can you be sure some Indian hasn't already thought of that?" she asked. "I mean, what if they expect us to be too smart to use the beaten path, so they've set up an ambush for any smarties trying to get by them some other way?"

Longarm chuckled. "Remind me to tell you the sad story of General George McClellan sometime. He was a gent who liked to consider every possible dirty trick the other side could possibly have in mind. He was bright as a button and kindly enough to design this good old army saddle I'm sitting right now. He managed to snatch defeat from the jaws of victory at Antietam by considering all the things Robert E. Lee might or might not be plotting, even as Lee's badly licked army was dragging itself from the field with all the fight knocked out of it. Never play chess when the other side is playing checkers, Steve. We got to get to Pumpkin Buttes *some* damned way. If them Indians have every way covered, they'll likely stop us. Since not even Red Cloud and the Lakota Confederacy out in full force could cover every infernal approach across miles and miles of nothing much, I doubt they'll even try. You got to spot folks on the High Plains before you can ambush 'em worth mention, and so far, I hope, we ain't been spotted."

She gulped hard and replied, "I hope so too. I confess it's a lot easier to feel the Indians are the ones being picked on when one's reading about it behind locked doors. Out here in the dark, in Indian country, I'm not so sure they can *all* be trusted as long as one's heart is in the right place."

He didn't think she'd want to hear where some Indians

considered the right place for an enemy's heart. He wasn't sure that yarn about Custer being found with his heart stuffed in his mouth was true in any case. Another old boy who'd been there said it had been his cock and balls, while the official army version, out of courtesy to the Widow Custer, involved the noble savages treating the body with the utmost respect. Everybody knew how much the Indians had loved old Yaller Hair. That was doubtless why they'd made him feel so much to home at Little Bighorn, about four or five days in the saddle to the north of those mysterious smoke signals.

Stephanie was going on and on about some horror tales she'd heard about white gals taken alive by Indians. He told her the tale of Quanah Parker's white mother, Cynthia Ann, knowing that was about as cheerful as such tales tended to turn out.

"Cynthia Ann was carried off by Comanche raiders who treated her decent enough, she told the Texas Rangers later. She was captured as a girl and adopted by a Comanche family. After she got big enough, Chief Peta Nocona come courting with honorable intentions and she married up with him willingly. They had three kids; the famous chief, Quanah; a younger brother called Puma or Pecos, depending on who you ask; and a daughter named Topasannah, who died as a baby shortly after the Rangers saved old Cynthia Ann, they said."

Stephanie frowned thoughtfully. "Is there any doubt they saved the poor woman from a fate worse than death, Custis?"

Longarm fished out a cheroot to chew, unlit, as he told her, "I wasn't there. So I just can't say why Cynthia Ann kept trying to run away and rejoin her sons and those other Comanche. She died before I ever got near Texas after the war. Some say she starved herself to death when her white relations locked her up to keep her decent. Others say she was simply taken by the same fever that killed her baby daughter. The only point to my telling you her tale is that things couldn't have been all bad for old Cynthia Ann as a captured white gal."

Stephanie sounded less than convinced as they rode on. She asked if he'd ever heard of Indians scalping white women.

He had. "There's nothing writ on stone. Mister Lo don't savvy rules and regulations the way we might, Steve. Tatanka

46

Yatanka, as they call Sitting Bull, is famous for treating captives as kind as if they were kissing cousins invited for supper, whilst old Tasunke Witco, or Crazy Horse, could shock other Indians with his inspired carvings. Some Indians don't scalp at all. Others make a religious rite out of it and consider a female scalp proof of bravery."

"How could any man consider it brave to mistreat a woman?" she asked indignantly.

He smiled thinly, not too surprised by her change in attitude toward Indians since first they'd met at a safer distance from those Indians. "It ain't fair to judge others by your own standards, Steve. Most Indians walk ahead of their women and children, not to be impolite but to protect 'em from anything mean along the trail ahead. As for it taking courage to scalp a woman, it reads a mite braver as soon as you consider the risks involved. You can jump another man most anywhere. You have to push your way all the way inside an enemy's quarters, past all the enemy defenses, to get at his womenfolk with your scalping knife."

Stephanie shuddered and said, "You've no idea how you're cheering me up with all this talk about quaint racial relationships. You say the Indians we have to worry about right now are Blackfoot? How do Blackfoot compare with Comanche or Sioux when it comes to making a lady feel welcome?"

They were topping another rise by now. He reined them in for a good look all around as he told her, "Siksika can be sort of sullen. But most I've met have been decent as most. Comanche are the only Horse Indians who act at all the way they're supposed to in those Wild West stories of Ned Buntline. Like Cheyenne, Cree, and other such Algonquin speakers, the so-called Blackfoot hold it's foolish not to fight sneaky and run away as soon as it looks as if you might get hurt."

She asked if he'd forgotten that old-timer who'd run away from Indians and still gotten hurt. He shook his head and replied, "That's what I just said. They had the advantage on him. They've yet to hit anybody serious in these parts. They've been playing it mighty safe, even for a small party of Siksika who have no damned business this far south to begin with."

He was about to heel his mount onward. Then he stared harder at a point of light off to their west. "That star's bright enough and yellow enough for the Dog Star, but what's it doing over yonder this far from the dog days of August?"

She opined all the stars in a mighty starry sky looked much the same to her that night. He shook his head and said, "That ain't no star. It's a campfire. About a mile the other side of that old Bozeman Trail. Nobody traveling along the wagon trace would be able to see it. We can just make it out from here because this rise is a tad higher than anything this side of yonder flickers."

She said she had no idea which tiny pinpoint of light they might be talking about. "Let's hope those Indians stay right where they are while we ride on then!"

He grimaced. "That ain't no Indian fire. It's too big and placed too dumb. We're a good mile east of the Bozeman Trail right now. That fool fire's as far off the trail to the west. So what kind of a blithering idiot could have lit things up so noticeably?"

"Where do you think you're going?" she protested, as she noticed the way he seemed to be leading them.

He told her, "I ain't just thinking, honey. Billy Vail sent me all this way to find out what in thunder might be going on. So let's go find out what's going on."

She softly wailed, "I don't want to get screwed and scalped by Blackfoot, damn it!"

He chuckled and replied, "Neither do I. I just now said that can't be any Indian fire. Meanwhile, at least two sets of hoofbeats trailed us out of Douglas, lost us in the dark, and could be laying for us most anywhere. That night fire's burning out of sight from the low-slung wagon trace ahead. I figure on swinging around to the north and easing in on it from the northwest."

She muttered, "Speak for yourself then. I'd forgotten those hired guns after you! This is getting downright scary, Custis!"

"I thought you wanted an exciting story for your newspaper. I don't mean to lead you into battle with nobody, honey. Once we've swung around the rascals, I'll leave you these ponies at a safe distance and sort of mosey in afoot. There's always the chance that innocent travelers are just camped stupid."

"Or not-so-innocent types are out to lure you like a moth

to their candle flame," she pointed out. "Have you thought of that?"

"Yep. But like I said, turning a checker game into a chess game can waste a heap of moves. I just told you I meant to move in on 'em sort of sneaky."

So that was the way they spent most of the next hour, walking their mounts around to the north, losing sight of the mysterious night fire for a time, and then picking it up again as they worked around the rises shielding its glow from the wagon trace they'd crossed along the way. Longarm made sure they were north-northwest of the flicker, now brighter than ever, before he reined in atop yet another rise to draw his Winchester from its boot and tell his worried companion, "I want you to stay here and hold these lead lines till I wave you in or signal you to run for it. You'll be able to see me afoot as long as I stay betwixt you and yonder glow. Any questions?"

She gulped and replied, "Yes. What happens to you if I ride off with these four ponies?"

"I may never speak to you again. I won't want you riding off unless it looks as if I've no chance of getting back here mighty sudden. We ain't got time to argue about it, Steve. Try to keep me in sight. Shift right or left to do so if you have to, and use your own judgment if you notice me getting into anything I can't get out of!"

As he dismounted and handed her the other reins as well she sobbed, "Custis, I'm scared!"

He didn't tell her that made two of them. He patted her denim-clad knee and said, "I'll be waving you in or running back this way any time now. Don't run off on me for no reason. But don't take chances neither."

Then he spun on one boot to head south-southeast toward that fool fire, numbly wondering why he suddenly felt like pissing, even though his mouth felt as if he hadn't had a drop to drink since New Year's.

As he strode toward the mysterious glow, it winked out ahead of him, or rather, he lost sight of it as he had to cross a wide shallow draw that put the next rise between him and whatever.

He eased up the next long slope, silent as any cat could

have managed, thanks to the soft spring sod underfoot. When he figured the girl he'd left a furlong or more back could make his outline out again, he waved back at her reassuringly, and moved on hunkered low over his Winchester until he stopped, his own eyes level with the crest of the rise and a clearer, or at any rate closer view of the campsite beyond.

He saw no mounts. He wasn't surprised. Lots of old boys knew about cottonwood browse in nearby draws. Two dark forms lay close to the fire. Nobody seemed to be on guard. But things were not always as they seemed. Longarm waited a spell, and when that didn't work he explored with his boot tips until he found a dried buffalo chip in the grass. He picked it up with his free hand and skimmed it out into the firelight to see who might notice.

Nobody seemed to as the pie-plate-sized slab of dung landed on edge to cartwheel on with at least enough noise to wake up your average cat. Anyone already awake should have surely heard the fool noise. So when nobody reacted, Longarm eased even closer, gun muzzle preceding as he braced for sudden noises himself.

But there weren't even any crackles from that stupidly bright fire. It appeared they'd actually brought along their own pressed-coal bricks made for dudes too lazy to rustle up firewood or dry chips on the trail. From the way the fool fire was still blazing, they'd heaped on way too many before turning in for the night.

If they'd really turned in.

Two tarps tossed over most anything could hide a multitude of sins. It was impossible to tell, by flickering firelight, whether either was breathing or not. It was said that he who hesitates is lost while fools rush in where angels fear to tread. At times like this it was easier to see how McClellan had felt at Antietam or how Custer had felt at Little Bighorn. Longarm knew some foxy grandpa could have that needlessly expensive fire baited with soapweed dummies. At the same time he knew he could be acting like a nervous nelly with the drop on a pair of total green-horns. He couldn't just stand there. So he commenced to circle and scout.

He knew he couldn't crab far to his right without the gal back yonder with the ponies losing sight of him against the firelight. He figured it would upset her even more to see him fall down full of lead. So he kept going, just outside the ruddy glow of the burning fuel bricks until, sure enough, on the far side, he came upon fresh horseshit and scuffed sod where at least two ponies had been hobbled to graze. Neither was there now.

He found the first body fifty yards further, spread-eagled on its back and naked as a jay. He could tell it had been a white man, despite the blood-red light, for the poor cuss had sported a heavy blond beard and doubtless a good head of hair, before someone had peeled his skull from the eyebrows up and back.

They'd cut off his privates and ripped out his guts as well. But more importantly, they'd cut his throat from ear to ear—as they were leaving, judging from the blood-blackened grass all about.

In sign talk you signified Lakota by cutting your own throat with a finger. By the same reasoning you indicated Cheyenne by pretending to slash your own hand. Longarm grumbled, "I reckon Siksika cut an occasional throat, pard. There's nothing in the constitution saying Mister Lo can't kill us any damn way he can get at us."

He moved on. The second body lay in the same undignified position and condition about ten yards to the east. Its throat was cut the same way. Someone had tried to light one of those patent bricks on the white boy's bare chest. But they'd burnt mostly hair before they'd settled for simply disemboweling and castrating him. They'd left his toeless and doubtless stinky socks on. There was no way to tell whether either had been wearing that big black Texas hat old Steve had spotted down Douglas way, but Longarm decided, "It still works. Local cowhands would have had no call to hunker just off the Bozeman Trail in times like these until someone else noticed their big dumb fire. A heap of street urchins from city slums take to the owlhoot trail in later years without ever learning too many country customs."

He kept circling, really on the prod now. When he cut the sign of unshod ponies, at least a dozen unshod ponies, in the sand of a nearby shallow wash, he figured the war party had dismounted there to do some foot patrolling of their own. He eased on soft and sneaky lest they still be about as he tried to put things together sensibly. Unless the Indians had left those dummies by the fire, in which case he and old Steve could be in a disgusting fix, those white boys had sort of outsmarted their own fool selves by baiting a trap for more modest prey than they'd attracted in the end.

He made it just about where he'd started, after circling the whole campsite. He waved at the unseen Stephanie and headed her way, musing half aloud, "If they were gunslicks laying for us, we were supposed to spot that fire. Anyone with my rep would be expected to scout the rises to either side and come in shooting as soon as I thought I had the drop on the two owlhoot riders they knew I was watching out for!"

He moved on, peering into the darkness ahead for some sign of the newspaper gal and those ponies as he decided, "One thing's for certain. Whoever was out to get me back in Douglas can't be in cahoots with them Siksika. So what might some white villain want with my poor ass, and what are them fool Siksika doing this far from the infernal Blackfoot agency up Montana way?"

He felt sure he was within earshot of Stephanie Chandler by this time. He called out, "Hey, Steve? Where are you at, honey? There ain't nobody we have to worry about around here now."

There was no answer. A big gray cat got up to turn around a time or two in Longarm's guts. He swallowed hard and moved on, eyes narrowed and Winchester ready for most anything until, at last, he stepped in fresh horseshit.

He called out, "It's me and this is no time to play kid games, honey. Those Indians we were jawing about have hit again, a heap closer, and I'd like to get us on down the road now if it's all the same with you."

There was no reply. He knew the flare of a match head could be seen at least three miles on a moonless night. He still needed more light on the subject. So he hunkered down to remove his Stetson and thumbnail a match alight under its flat crown. It only took a few seconds, staring soberly down with the Winchester across his thighs, to determine she'd lit out at a lope with all four ponies to strand him a good day's ride from anywhere—and one hell of a lot longer to walk!

52

He shook out the match, rose, and commenced to walk anyway, aiming north by the stars. For he wanted to put as much distance as possible between his own hide and those mutilated white boys before the sun came up, as it had to, to catch him alone out here on the High Plains, on foot, with at least a dozen Horse Indians out for blood!

Chapter 7

By the time the sky to his east was pearling from inky black to dishwater gray, Longarm was sincerely sorry he'd ever met Miss Stephanie Chandler, and mighty glad he'd done so in low-heeled army boots. For even so, he felt sure he'd trudged at least as far as the Canadian border, and where in the hell was that trail town he'd figured as no more than a day's ride up the trail?

He was following the Bozeman off to one side, across more rolling grass that offered a man afoot with a Winchester, Colt, and double derringer at least a chance. Meanwhile all three guns had been gaining weight alarmingly, and aside from feeling tuckered, he was hungry as a Chinese village and thirsty enough to drink water.

But first things coming first, he had to find cover, good cover, before it got much lighter in these parts. He was already trying to stay off the skyline, knowing how far moving dots on the horizon could be seen against the big naked sky of the High Plains. Following a north-trending contour line below the crests of the grass-covered rises made for way more walking and kept him from seeing too far ahead, but when he considered how many infernal Indians could be staring right back at him, he found it easy to resist any temptations.

54

He felt sure he'd been following a wise policy when, just about the time he started to see colors again, he heard the not-too-far crackle of small-arms fire and naturally headed that way, however slowly.

Old soldiers learn to advance on the sounds of gunfire for more than one good reason. To begin with, old soldiers learn to act contrary, knowing there are whole chapters of military science devoted to killing green troops involving the natural instincts of humankind. Since nine out of ten rational beings tended to head for other parts when they heard guns going off, old soldiers assumed nobody was baiting a trap for them with all that noise, and better yet, there were usually two sides in a firefight. So some of that gunfire figured to be friendly.

Sounds could carry oddly across rolling prairie. But Longarm was pretty sure the fuss was taking place a mite to his left, or west of his original course in line with the Bozeman Trail. He was trudging up a soapweed-dotted slope when the sounds of gunfire suddenly ceased, and knowing what might happen next, he ran for the biggest clump of soapweed at hand and flattened out amid the eighteen-inch spines of park-bench green just in time.

They'd have spotted him for certain if they'd been expecting anything important on the far slope they came boiling over the crest with the rising sun in their eyes. Longarm didn't get a good look at them either, as he tried to get way flatter with his cheek pressed to the sod between two soapweed clumps. But he made it at least a dozen befeathered assholes laughing and yelling as they tore by, avoiding his spiny but mighty meager cover without having to study on it. A buckskin pony that had come perilously close to stomping on his head had been painted with the black hindquarter stripes of a leader, and the yellow hand prints had spelled Heap Bad Injun as well. An Indian slapped a palm dipped in red on the hide of a pony he'd killed somebody with. A yellow palm print meant some poor bastard taken alive, and hence more to brag about. Nobody with a lick of sense got taken alive by *any* Horse Indians. The Siksika, for all their generous manners in peacetime, were said to be able to keep a captive alive as long, and as uncomfortably, as anyone this side of, say, a Sonora Yaqui. Nobody could torture as exquisitely as a Yaqui.

But Longarm didn't desire the chance to compare the techniques of any nation. So he lay doggo for what felt like a million years until, at last, he couldn't hear hoofbeats no matter how hard he pressed his ear to the sod. Then he took a deep breath and gingerly raised his bare head to see nothing but maybe some dust haze against the glaring sunrise those Indians had ridden into.

He put his hat back on and rose to get at least one more rise between himself and those happy-go-lucky sons of bitches. He was pretty sure he'd find somebody alive as well as white up ahead. He put what he'd just heard and seen as a dawn surprise attack that hadn't surprised anyone. The Indians had likely circled a mite, smoking things up in their usual custom, till the light had gotten too good and the shooting too serious for their taste. Then, lacking cover to begin with, and siege warfare not being their style in any case, they'd simply ridden off to try somewhere else.

What in thunder they were trying to prove took way more study. He knew for certain now there were really Indians acting up. After that, it still made little sense, even when one tried to walk a ways in blue beaded moccasins. For this had never been Siksika territory. The Lakota had taken this Powder River range away from Shoshoni, Salish, Utes, and such to lose it in turn to white settlers. Pissed-off Lakota or even Shoshoni visiting their old neighborhood made sense. Nobody from any of the Blackfoot nations did. There were plenty of whites worth raiding, on both sides of the border, up around the big Blackfoot agency between Heart Butte and the Milk River.

As the sunrise smote his back, Longarm knew the day was shaping up as a scorcher. He peeled off his coat and loosely knotted the sleeves around his neck to let some air get at his bare shirt sleeves at least. It wasn't smart to spend time on the skyline. So as he topped the next rise he went right over it and downslope a ways to pause and gaze about on that side. The morning sun was gleaming off the stationary vanes of a sunflower windmill less than a quarter mile ahead. Thin blue wisps of dung smoke were rising from behind that same long grassy ridge. Longarm nodded and muttered, "Now that we know who them Indians were shooting at, let's find out if they hit anybody."

He almost got hit himself as he was crossing the shallow draw between rises. For even though he crabbed to one side as he spied a cottonball of gunsmoke from a distant clump of soapweed, the bullet and its whip-crack report made his heart skip a beat when they reached his immediate vicinity.

Longarm held his own fire. It wasn't easy. Then a plaintive youthful voice called out, "You ain't no Blackfoot, are you?"

To which Longarm could only call back, "I ain't an Indian of any sort, as anyone can plainly see."

So the skinny kid in bib overalls rose from his own clump of soapweed with a Spencer repeater, held polite, to yell, "You'd best get on up here then. We was just hit by Blackfoot and they're likely still about!"

As Longarm strode upslope to join the kid on the rise he called, "I doubt it. They were headed somewheres in a hurry when they like to run me over a couple of furlongs to the east. Who says they had to be Blackfoot? No offense, but you just now took *me* for one of 'em and I ain't wearing one damn feather!"

The kid smiled sheepishly. "Crow Mary says they was Blackfoot and she ought to know. Blackfoot kilt her daddy when he was scouting for the Seventh Cav that time."

Longarm didn't ask what time they were talking about. Time had stopped in these parts for the Seventh Cav on June 25, 1876, and would never commence again till they got to butcher some Indians, a heap of Indians, to make up for Little Bighorn. He didn't ask what a Crow gal might be doing on the Wasichu side in a fight with Siksika either as he followed the young rifleman up and over the rise. An Absaroke named Mary had to be a Christian convert, and they'd just agreed her dad had thrown in with the Great White Father.

Aside from getting a lot of Red Cloud's old hunting grounds for their own grand Crow Reserve, the Absaroke had heaps of other privileges denied more surly nations. They got to live as red or white as they might see fit, on or off the B.I.A. books if

57

they preferred to work for real money instead of spitting and whittling around some agency between allotment days.

As he followed the kid over the crest of the rise, Longarm saw at a glance what all the fuss had been about. That windmill rose at one corner of a good-sized pole corral inhabited by no less than three dozen head of riding stock. Less important to any passing Horse Indians, there was a sod-roofed house and a half-dozen outbuildings, the whole spread surrounded by three strands of spiderwebby bob-wire on skinny patent poles of notched angle iron. Seeing they'd fenced in their full quarter-section claim, Longarm commented, "It was a good thing they hit you early in the morning, before you'd turned your stock out to graze all that prime buffalo grass you just improved."

The kid chuckled and replied, "That's for durned sure. Crow Mary says her kind ain't used to Mister Joseph Glidden's wondrous invention. You should have seen that one old buck go ass over tea kettle when he tried to ride betwixt two posts on his painted pony!"

Longarm had to smile at the picture as they trudged down the far slope, digging in their heels. For it was easy to see how suddenly a mount might get going towards that unimpressive fence line, and so the hank of feather-braided black hair, whether man or beast, made for easy sign to read as it swayed in the gentle breeze from a top strand.

The kid went on. "They meant to take us by surprise by dashing in with the sunrise ahint 'em. Have you ever awoke to the dulcet sounds of three or four Indians hitting a bob-wire fence at the same time? By the time they'd remounted and gathered their wits we was wide awake at all the loopholes, and they must have figured that out after they'd circled us a time or two. Aunt Nelly says she's sure she kilt at least one of the red rascals with her pepper box. For she was blazing like anything as one rid right along the fence line making faces at us."

Longarm was too polite to comment as they approached the fence line under discussion. The nearest sod wall rose a good ten yards from the far side of the wire, a possible but hardly easy pistol shot, and none of those Indians he'd spied further east had been hit bad enough to notice in any case. A pallid dishwater blonde was staring out a rifle slit cut through the otherwise blank wall facing the fence line. As they rolled through the two top strands Longarm pulled that feathery length of braided black hair from the barbs it had been snagged by. As they circled around the soddy he saw it was really horse hair, and likely torn from the ass end of some show-off's real scalp lock. White ladies of fashion had hardly invented the notion of improving on nature with more hair than they might be able to grow all by their fool selves.

The three coup feathers braided in with sinew and red trading post yarn bragged on doing wonders. Two were real eagle feathers. The third was a goose quill with its tip dipped in black paint to make up for any current shortage of eagles. That one had yellow dots along one vane to signify the taking of four prisoners alive, the poor bastards. The red spots and chevrons on the real eagle feathers recorded enemies simply killed or killed with trimmings in close encounters. Folks who bragged with feathers counted it braver to slap a man's face up close than to shoot him dead from behind at a safe distance, which sounded fair enough as soon as one studied on it.

An older man with some resemblance to the ragged-ass kid met them on the far side to nod curtly at Longarm and say, "We've already et, but there's some coffee left and we'd best all get inside afore them Blackfoot sons of bitches come back!"

Longarm's stomach was really growling by now. But he knew nobody would refuse food to a stranger in these parts if they had any to spare. So he said coffee sounded swell and followed the old nester and his boy inside. Longarm had to duck under the door lintel as he did so. Sod walls always settled some, and in this case they'd started with a lower roof than they might have.

Inside the nearly windowless soddy it took a few minutes for Longarm's eyes to adjust to the gloom. By the time they did, he'd been led to a plank table and plunked down on a three-legged stool so a dark figure could serve him a tin cup of weak coffee and, despite what the master of the house had just said, a slice of corn bread with no butter.

Both tasted grand after all that time with neither food nor

drink. When he said that, he was served a second cup despite the warning hiss from some less hospitable female in the darker shadows. The man of the house sat across from Longarm and growled, "I'll have what's left of that." Then he told Longarm, more gently, he was Silas Price, and had been grasshoppered out down near Trinidad. "I ain't never going to try and grow barley in this here Great American Desert," he said. "Nothing grows half as good as the natural grass in these parts, and so now I mean to raise heaps of expensive riding stock for the cattle outfits springing up all about."

Longarm identified himself, flashing his badge before he added, "I seem to have come to the right place then. As you may have noticed, I find myself afoot. The how and why of it is a long sad story. Suffice it to say I got to get on up to Pumpkin Buttes, and I've already walked farther than even my cruel boss ever told me to. So what would you ask for the hire of a pony and stock saddle, long enough to get me to the nearest town?"

Silas Price frowned dubiously. "I just can't see hiring a horse or saddle with horse-raiding Blackfoot right outside my very door, Deputy Long. If you'd like to *buy,* I could let you have a fine fast gelding with the saddle throwed in for, oh, let's say an even hundred, cash on the barrel head."

Longarm whistled. "I'm sure you have the barrel head, but that's a heap of cash. I only make a little over fifty a month."

The older man shrugged and insisted, "I never asked how much Uncle Sam paid you. You asked how much I wanted, see?"

Longarm could see indeed now. He wrinkled his nose and muttered, "Serves me right for intimating I was riding for such a rich uncle. You'll take a written I.O.U. for that much, I hope?"

Silas Price shook his head smugly and repeated, "Cash on the barrel head. I'm an old army man with some experience waiting for government checks. I'd have to charge you ten times as much, risking real horse flesh against government paper signed by anyone as low on the totem pole as you— no offense."

Longarm was tempted, two ways. He actually had close to a hundred in cash on him, and nobody would ever believe he'd signed an I.O.U. for a thousand dollars of his own free will, cold sober. But he still drained the last of the weak coffee and asked the assemblage at large how far the next town might really be.

Nobody answered. He sensed they all knew Silas Price didn't want them to. It was easy enough to figure why. It likely meant the distance wasn't as impossible as the country slicker wanted him to suspect it might be. So seeing his whistle was wet enough to smoke now, Longarm got out a couple of cheroots, silently offered one to the cuss across the table, and seeing old Silas was willing to smoke and screw at the same time, struck a light for them both.

By the sudden flare he was able to confirm that the white woman and her four half-grown kids were ugly, while the Indian girl who'd been more decent about serving a stranger was younger and better-looking than "Crow Mary" sounded. Her hair was neatly braided and her youthful figure filled her blue print Mother Hubbard out mighty interestingly. As he finished lighting his own cheroot and shook the match out Longarm said, "Let's study on what I might be riding through before we argue whether I can afford it or not."

He took that hank of horse hair from where he'd draped it across his thighs, and placed it on the table by his tin cup, saying, "These coup feathers look like some a Lakota was sporting when I dropped him up near the Rosebud in the summer of '77. I've mostly worked with Siksika or Blackfoot in peacetime, when one pays less attention to feathers, but don't Siksika go in more for weasel tails, squirrel tails, and such than feathers?"

The Indian girl said, "We call the Blackfoot Siha Sapa in my tongue. It means the same thing. Maybe some of them wear weasel tails. Maybe some of them carry umbrellas. They are all *witco* as dogs with the foaming sickness. But their feather talk is the same as everyone else's. What good would it be to boast of bad things you did to my people, or even Utes, if nobody but your own nation could read your feathers?"

Longarm nodded and said, "Just covering all bets, ma'am. You ain't the first one to offer an informed opinion as to the nation of these otherwise mysterious scamps."

Silas Price asked what was so mysterious about wild Indians, adding, "They was after our ponies, right outside, not one full hour ago, cuss their greasy red hides!"

Crow Mary added, "I shot at them too. They were Siha Sapa. Their leader rode a bay army mount with many coup marks, many. Its tail was knotted to show it carried its rider along the trail of death. There were circles around its eyes to make it see like Owl, and there were red hands and yellow horseshoes, many, to show—"

"I know how to read coup marks," Longarm told her, scowling at the glowing tip of his cheroot. "All them signs of which we speak are Lakota as well. So no offense, but how come everyone but me is so certain they're Blackfoot?"

Crow Mary sounded disgusted as she snapped, "Because that is what they were, Wasichu Witco! Siha Sapa killed my father. Siha Sapa tried to carry me away when I was only nine summers old, the baby-raping dog-fuckers!"

The white woman in the corner gasped and protested, "Not in front of the little ones, you savage!"

To which Crow Mary replied with a shrug, "None of your stepchildren are much younger than you, and you shouldn't make them help with the chores on a stud spread if you don't want them to know about fucking."

"That'll be enough of that, Mary," Silas Price said, wearily, as at least two of the kids laughed outright.

The Indian girl said, "Don't ask me to talk about dog-fucking Blackfoot then."

Longarm said soothingly, "I'll take your word they were Siksika or, all right, Siha Sapa, if you'll be good enough to offer an educated guess as to what they might be doing so far from home."

Silas Price snorted and said, "That's easy. Blackfoot have ever been infamous horse thieves."

"Not in these parts," Longarm insisted, pointing with his cheroot as he continued. "There's the Wind River Shoshone Agency due west and then some. There's the Pine Ridge Agency even further, to the east. Miss Mary here would be off the Big Horn Crow or Absaroke Agency up the Bozeman Trail to the north. That leaves us the smaller Cheyenne and Arapaho reserves, such as Tongue River. There just ain't supposed to be no infernal Blackfoot south of the Teton River, which is where we are with many a day's ride left over!"

Everyone there agreed it was a caution how far Blackfoot seemed willing to ride just to steal horses. Longarm grumbled, "They have to have better reasons than that. There's riding stock to steal all over the West. But so far, nobody's spotted any painted Blackfoot as far south as Douglas or as far north as Buffalo, that big trail town up closer to Miss Mary's agency."

He took a thoughtful drag on his cheroot and got back to his feet. "Meanwhile, I ain't about to get it on in to Pumpkin Buttes sitting down on a stool. So I'd best get going if I mean to go."

Silas Price swore under his breath and got to his own feet. "You can't go on without you let me sell you that horse and saddle, Deputy Long. Pumpkin Buttes is over ten miles up the trail, and even if it wasn't, there's wild Indians all about!"

Longarm smiled thinly and replied, "I was sort of hoping it was within easy walking distance. I generally worry about how wild anyone might or might not be when I meet up with 'em. Those old boys who just hit you were riding lickety-split to the east when last I saw 'em, and so, since that town's just over the horizon to the north-northwest, I'd best get cracking whilst the cracking's good."

He shifted his Winchester back to his left hand to open the door and let himself out. Old Silas and most of his brood seemed to want some fresh air as well. The would-be pony monger decided he'd take an I.O.U. for a hundred, after all.

Longarm chuckled fondly and said, "I'd best not. My office might not honor an expense chit for that little. Seeing as you need the business and it could take me more than three hours to stride ten miles afoot, I'll give you five dollars, cash, for the use of a fair mount till, say, the end of the week. I'll even pay someone in Pumpkin Buttes to return it no later than Monday afternoon if I can't deliver it in person for any reason."

The older man shook his head stubbornly and insisted, "I won't hire. You got to buy. A fair pony with a good-enough saddle and bridle throwed in? Fifty dollars. Take it or leave it."

Longarm left it. As he strode for the fence line Silas Price tagged along, protesting. "You drive a damned hard bargain but, all right, how's about twenty-five in hard coinage or, hell, paper money if it's all you got?"

Longarm rolled through the fence, gripping his cheroot in a wolfish grin as he decided. "Remember me when next you feel you have a poor wayfaring stranger by the balls, amigo. I was ready to treat you more than fair when first you saw fit to skin me so greedy. I thought you and your kin might be hard up for cash here, when all you offered was dishwater and dry pone. But now that I see you're a skinflint out to get rich quick, I'll just get out of your way and let you get right to it."

"Aw, come on, I'll hire you a damned old pony for a dollar a day," he said, now sort of desperate. But Longarm just kept going, not looking back, all the way up that long shallow rise between the stud spread by the trail and some higher and maybe safer walking. Silas Price was aptly named, he thought to himself as he left the spread behind.

As he trended along the ridge to the east of the old trail he could see for miles, or at least he could see anything that might want to be seen for miles. One of the reasons it had taken so much effort to clear old Red Cloud—Company off this Powder River range was the simple fact that one could hide a whole Indian village less than a full mile off in such apparently empty but treacherously rolling country. He knew he'd be harder to spot at a distance if he worked his way to town by way of as many draws as he might manage. He knew it would take him way longer and leave him at a hell of a disadvantage if he was spotted too. So he followed a level contour line, keeping his head off the skyline, of course, but staying high enough to spot anyone coming his way long before they might get to him across open shortgrass. Meanwhile, if only he could spy some prairie turnips, wild onions, or even milkweed buds, for Gawd's sake, he might not starve to death after all.

He didn't spot any edible weeds, damn all grazing animals, but now he could keep the actual Pumpkin Buttes in sight all the time as he trudged onward with the sun rising ever warmer and not half way to the zenith yet.

Opening the front of his vest helped, but not enough. He took his watch and derringer from their vest pockets and shoved them both in a rear pants pocket. Then he removed the vest entirely to roll up with his frock coat. By lashing them in a neat roll with the aid of the otherwise useless shoestring tie—which they'd saddled him with since President Hayes and his fancy first lady, Lemonade Lucy, had gotten so high-toned—he was able to free most of his hickory shirt to scatter more of his body heat as the shirt flapped damply in time with his long-legged strides. He cursed himself for not having a sling attached to the infernal Winchester, and finally settled for carrying his rolled coat and vest sort of hobo style, horse-collared over his shouldered rifle.

Those distant Pumpkin Buttes, named more for their color than shape, stayed just as distant as he strode on and on, wondering why he'd ever thought this might be a good lesson for that greedy nester back yonder.

He kept going, picturing the steak smothered in chili and eggs he meant to order as soon as he got to town, if ever he got to any damn town.

Then far more steak than he'd had in mind came over the rise ahead to snort and paw the earth as it regarded him with some surprise.

The old bull buffalo had to be a rogue. For the critters roamed in herds unless they'd been driven away by other buff for being so cranky. Longarm knew better than to turn away or even stop. He could only keep going at the same steady stride, hoping this particular brute had more than a normal bovine brain to go with its fifteen hundred pounds or so of mighty moveable mass.

There was some debate as to whether a buffalo or longhorn won first prize for lethal stupidity. Both tended to shy away from anything as big as a horse and rider coming their way on four hooves. Neither seemed to show much respect for anything as puny-looking to them as a man on foot. Longarm changed course just enough so he was striding straight at the big shaggy brute, hoping that might make him seem a mite more ominous.

It didn't. The old rogue lowered its massive head and gathered its big hooves together as its tail shot straight up, inspiring Longarm to break stride and swing his Winchester around to port arms, letting his rolled coat and vest land anywhere they might have a mind to. For if that lonesome loco critter wasn't fixing to charge, it was a lying son of a bitch!

65

It charged. Longarm stood his ground and fired from the hip, to scare the buff, not to hit it. For no .44-40 Winchester round was about to stop a charging bull buffalo, and the brute was already mad enough at him for no good reason.

Four gunshots in a rapid-fire row didn't even make the big buff blink as far as Longarm could tell. Beef cows were easier to spook with loud noises. Buffalo hunters worried more about the herd catching wind of humankind, and claimed they could fire into a herd all day as long as the wind didn't shift and their chosen targets dropped calm and serene. Longarm forced himself to stand still, if not serene, and sidestepped at the last possible moment to let the massive beast pound by, close enough to feel the heat of its hairy hide.

Then they were facing one another again and, seeing the shaggy son of a bitch was fixing to come charging back at him, Longarm levered another round in the chamber and, this time, aimed to drop the damn fool buff before it could get moving good again.

That didn't work either. Getting peppered with man-stopping slugs as it charged couldn't be doing the old rogue any good, and it would likely lie down and die from the fusillade in a day or so. But that was small consolation to Longarm as, this time, he dodged to the right of the charging bull while, sure enough, that massive head hooked to its left with a big black horn.

Longarm didn't know how one went about fooling a buff once it commenced to study on one's dance steps. He knew Mex bullfighters refused to get into the ring with a critter who'd been fought before and spared. He knew the most dangerous bovine of all was a dairy cow with a mean streak because it was even more used to the way a human being got about on two legs. As the bull buff slid to a dusty stop about twenty yards off and spun around to take another bearing on its chosen victim, Longarm knew he only had a few seconds to decide which way to dodge this time. Was a buffalo smart enough to sense that a man might be smart enough to dodge the same way twice, in hopes a buff was smart enough to anticipate . . . and Jesus H. Christ, here it was coming again, shaking its big head like an infernal water spaniel as if it were out to gore the whole world!

Then the rogue buff spun on a dime to tear downslope with its big eyes rolling and its muzzle drooling slobber as Longarm, sensing hoofbeats behind him, spun and dropped to one knee to train the muzzle of his man-stopping Winchester on the one Indian and two Indian ponies coming at him lickety-split.

Chapter 8

Longarm held his fire. It wasn't easy. But he was glad he had as soon as he was sure that it was Crow Mary from the Price spread, riding a buckskin and leading a paint she had on a long lead of braided rawhide. She was riding astride with her calico skirts hiked up around her hips and her long bare legs exposed above her striped socks and mail-order high-buttons. As she reined in near Longarm she said, poker-faced, "I am on my way home by way of Pumpkin Buttes. If you know how to ride bareback you might want to keep me company that far."

Longarm bent to regather his rolled-up tweeds from the grass and moved to the right side of the paint, saying, "I ain't as scared of this old *tasunke* as that old *tatanka* was—unless you stole it, that is."

As he mounted Indian-style, from the right, the Indian gal said, soberly, "It is the custom for Navajo women to steal. Absaroke girls are not raised that way. The Prices still owe me money. I had these ponies when I came to work for them. I don't think Silas Price ever meant to pay me. I don't think I want to work for Wasichu anymore. I think I should go back to my agency. The agents lie to us too, but at least they give us *something* once in a while and we don't have to do anything for anyone we don't like."

Longarm shifted his rifle and pack to ride more securely across his thighs as he sat the paint bareback. It wasn't true that Indians preferred to ride this way. They made fair saddles to augment those they could trade for or take by force, with a cavalry saddle taken in battle the top brag. When Indians rode bareback it was for the same reason anyone else might have. You had to ride bareback if you didn't have a saddle. Like farm kids, Indians were more used to it and could do it a tad better than your average city dude. After that most any rider with his or her feet braced in stirrups and a rump braced by even an English-style cantle had any bareback rider beat all hollow, which was why they'd invented saddles to begin with.

As he gathered in the lead line to coil it and use it as a rein end, Longarm asked if Silas Price owed Crow Mary enough to make it worth his while as a lawman. Riding on with her he explained, "As a federal lawman I don't have the power to collect local debts, as a rule. On the other hand, it's a federal offense to cheat a ward of the federal government, and you could surely pass for a full-blooded ward, no offense."

She smiled wistfully and replied, "I used to think I'd rather be a Wasichu girl. I thought you people treated your women better than my people. Now that I have worked for more than one Wasichu family I know better. I was thinking about going home before you came along this morning. When I saw you seemed to have a good heart as well as both a Colt and Winchester, I wondered how I was going to get you to take me with you. When I saw you would rather walk than let yourself be cheated, I saw this chance to ride with you."

Longarm cocked one eyebrow. "So you did, and we seem to be riding farther from the Price spread by the minute. So about them back wages, if you'd like me to help you collect 'em . . ."

"They offered me a dollar a week and I've worked for them almost a full month," She told him.

To which he could only reply, "I'd rather just slip you five or ten and not waste the time, if it's all the same with you. I was hoping to make it in to Pumpkin Buttes this side of noon, after which I hope you understand we ain't exchanged no eternal vows."

She nodded, sadly. "I know you will only be riding with me as far as the next settlement. I won't be able to go on from there before I pick up some trail supplies and at least one blanket. With those Blackfoot out this spring, I'll want to hide by day and ride by night once I leave Pumpkin Buttes. Would you like me to earn all that money after we get to town, or might you feel funny taking an Absaroke girl into a hotel room with you?"

He blinked and said he hadn't really studied ahead that far. So she demurely replied, "There is a wooded draw running across the trail about a mile on. If you ride up it a little ways you come upon a shady clearing where the the love-grass sod is soft and springy."

He might have responded to such an invitation one way or the other. But there were times to talk dirty and there were times to ride like hell, and when a dozen-odd riders in feathers and paint came boiling over a rise at you, all yelling and whooping at once, the last thing you felt like talking about had to be love grass!

Crow Mary was already lighting out the other way, lashing her pony too hard to require further instructions. So Longarm pegged a wild shot at the mounted skirmish line and lit out after her aboard the paint, hoping their two ponies were fresher at least. For after that the Indians had the edge.

Crow Mary wouldn't have known so much about the way ahead if she hadn't been over it a time or more while working for the Prices. So he let her take the lead and didn't argue when they tore down the far slope, across the wagon ruts of the Bozeman Trail at an acute angle, and up another long grassy slope as, behind them, guns commenced to crackle and puffs of mustard-colored dust rose from the prairie sod all around. Gripping his Winchester atop his tweeds and across his thighs with his rein hand, Longarm drew his double-action Colt .44-40 with his right and half turned as he tore on to empty it in hopes of getting the Indians to treat him and the lady he was escorting with more respect.

It just inspired them to whoop louder and blaze away faster with their own hardware. Then ahead of him, Longarm saw Crow Mary's pony going ass over tea kettle while the girl, one hell of a horsewoman, landed on her feet, running, till she hooked a damned high heel on something and went sprawling up the slope from her dying pony.

70

Longarm growled, "Aw, shit!" while he hauled hard on his own one line to slide his paint to a halt near the gal as she struggled to rise.

It would have been a hard row to hoe had he been riding with a regular rig. Now, without a bit in its mouth, the damned paint felt free to keep going as far and as fast as it might want, and with a dozen mounted Indians screaming at it all at once the paint wanted to go far and fast indeed. So Longarm simply rolled off to land on his side and roll over on his gut and elbows near the Indian gal as she gasped, "Now I know you've gone *witco*! But give me a gun and maybe we can give them a good fight!"

He handed her his emptied revolver and a fistful of fresh rounds as he cranked one into the chamber of his Winchester, dully trying to recall how many he'd already wasted on that fucking buffalo. He said, "I got a derringer in my hip pocket, with a shot for both of us when you figure we'll need 'em. You'd be the better judge of that, no offense."

Then he fired, prone, hitting the Indian pony he'd been aiming for, and then spinning its rider like a top with a second well-aimed shot as the redskin rose from the grass, cussing and shaking his own befeathered rifle.

The sudden display of mighty fine markmanship inspired the other Indians to whirl their ponies and put some distance between themselves and their intended victims. Sprawled beside him, Crow Mary popped the sixth fresh round in Longarm's Colt and chortled, "*Wa heya!* That was shooting to count coup on! But they are still cowards, cowards, to be stopped so easy!"

He smiled thinly and replied, "Let's not be too hard on the boys, you bloodthirsty little gal. They know any fair shot-firing from the prone position has the edge in a rifle fight. Meanwhile, there's still ten or eleven of 'em if they'd like to dismount and return the favor at long range."

She pointed out they just seemed to be sitting their mounts at the limits of easy shooting, holding some sort of mounted powwow. So he said calmly, "Give 'em time. The side on the attack always has the damn initiative, meaning they get to decide what happens next. They can see they got us pinned down on a wide-open slope with most of the whole damned day left."

She sighed. "I know. I'm already getting thirsty. If it was closer to sundown we could at least hope to make a break for that wooded draw I was telling you about, remember?"

He let go of the forestock of the Winchester to pat her cotton-clad rump reassuringly, knowing such gestures hardly counted now. "May as well wish for that hotel bed, as long as you're at it, Miss Mary. Shade trees ain't much use after dark, and if there was any cover at all betwixt us and those Blackfoot, they'd likely be working closer by now."

She hissed, "One comes! Alone! Listen, he is singing his death song!"

Longarm patted her rump again and let go to get a better grip on his Winchester as the lone Indian rode up the long gentle slope toward them—in point of fact, toward the one Indian Longarm had already downed. The singing rider was young, but two black circles painted on his bare tawny torso showed where he'd been hit by bullets in the past. The red and yellow coup stripes down his bare arms bragged on enemies who'd had worse luck with him. Crow Mary murmured, "His song says his medicine is good and all four of his ghosts are brave. He says all men die and that he'd just as soon die well now as later, old and weak with your kind laughing at him."

Longarm frowned thoughtfully, picking up just a word or two here and there as the mighty brave, or just plain stupid young cuss, sang on. Longarm knew sign and at least a few words of all the main dialects. He muttered, "Correct me if I'm wrong, but ain't that bird singing in Lakota, Miss Mary?"

She nodded and replied, "Of course. How else would I know what he was singing? My people are enemies of the Lakota you call Sioux, but in the beginning we were the bird people of the Hidasta Lakota. I don't know why you call us Crows."

Longarm said, "I don't either. Let's stick to Blackfoot. I've worked with Blackfoot before. They talk an Algonquin dialect, related to Arapaho, Cheyenne, and such. So how come that Blackfoot's singing in Lakota?"

She shrugged. "I don't know. Maybe that is why he sounds so much like a frog. Don't you want to shoot him?"

Longarm softly muttered, "Ain't sure. I'm trying to figure just what in thunder he might be up to. He ain't their leader, if all them black stripes on that other pony mean anything."

She wrinkled her nose and said, "Of course he's not a leader. He's a suicide rider, out to die or make a name for himself while he is still very young." She drew a bead with the sixgun in her own dainty hands, adding, "I think I'd rather see him die."

But Longarm snapped, "Don't! He's not after us right now. He's after that older brave I dropped out yonder. Our own troopers consider that a point of honor as well."

She insisted, "Kill him! If he recovers a fallen comrade from right in our sights, he will gain so much medicine all the girls will love him and all the men will hate him!"

Longarm chuckled. "Now that'd really make me feel sorry for all of 'em. But if he challenges their leader, dumb moves might end up helping us."

The Indian girl beside him brightened. "Oh, I see. You want him to do something his leader was afraid to do, and live. Before I worked for an army wife at Fort Laramie I would not have understood. You people are so treacherous when it comes to making war. You win all the time because you just don't care what anybody else thinks of you!"

The young Indian dismounted and, still singing, picked up his dead comrade. He had to stop singing and grunt a lot instead before he had the limp and messy corpse draped over an angular rawhide saddle, face down. Then the pony's owner led it downslope a few paces, turned to face Longarm and the girl, and yelled at them defiantly. According to Crow Mary, it was as dirty as anything she'd ever heard. She refused to translate in detail, but he got the impression it involved white men and their mothers in mighty undignified positions.

Longarm said, "I'd best send him on his way with good medicine. Feel free to join in, but in the name of your Wakan Tanka don't *hit* the silly little bastard!"

She laughed and said she followed his sneaky drift. So together, they dusted the leggings of that strolling Indian good while, to his dubious credit, he never flinched once. They peppered the prairie till Longarm decided it was time to quit while they were still ahead and reload. As they were doing so, the Indian gal warned, "They're really going to torture us now. We killed one of them. Then we showed how much medicine that other one has."

73

Longarm shrugged. "They might settle for just carving on me. You're a pretty little thing, and with any luck we've got at least two of 'em arguing about next moves now."

She sighed. "Oh, shit. They're forming up for another charge, and this time, they'll probably circle to fire on us from all sides at once. Promise you'll kill me when the time comes?"

He said he'd try as, sure enough, the befeathered sons of bitches began to spread out downslope with that one on the striped army bay still yelling officious orders.

Then, without warning and with almost fatal results to his own fool self, another mounted Indian tore over the rise they were on from the *north* to whip past Longarm and the Indian gal, yelling fit to bust about Wasichu, heaps of Wasichu, as close as Longarm could make out. Then they were all lighting out to the east in a cloud of dust as Crow Mary explained, "That was a scout they had over by that wooded draw I told you about. He just spotted a cavalry troop, or a big posse, coming this way!"

Longarm laughed weakly and said, "That's likely why they went the other way. We'd still best get our own selves somewheres way less exposed, lest they circle back."

As he rose and helped her to her feet, she asked why on earth the frightened Blackfoot would want to do that. Longarm hooked an elbow through his rolled-up coat and vest and headed down to where the dead Indian's dead pony still lay, muttering, "If it was safe to say what such old boys might or might not do, George Armstrong Custer might still be with us today."

She asked why, in that case, the two of them seemed to be headed the same way as those recently vanished Blackfoot. He bent over a few yards from the dead pony to pick up a beaded moccasin, stained a dull shade of dark blue, likely with some sort of berry juice. He said, "I wanted to make sure. Am I right in saying your word *sapa* can mean either blue or black, depending?"

She nodded. "Of course. It took me a long time to understand what you people meant when you said the two shades of *sapa* were two different colors. You say pink when you mean a light shade of *luta*, or red, too. Yet you still lump many colors, many, into your one word brown."

Longarm said, "I've used that point myself in explaining some of your notions to my own kind. If it's any comfort, Navajo feel just as certain blue and green are two shades of the same color, but they agree with us that black ain't blue."

Tossing the black-or blue-stained moccasin aside, it being sort of stinky once you'd studied it, Longarm swung the muzzle of his Winchester upslope to the north and added, "We'd best go meet them other Wasichu, or failing that, at least get into that infernal town some time this summer. I'm beginning to fell like old Coronado searching for them Seven Cities of Gold in the Great American Desert, and I know for certain there's a real place calt Pumpkin Buttes!"

Crow Mary assured him they were headed the right direction and that it wasn't too far to hope for supper in town, at least, whether they made it by noon or not. Then she pointed at the horizon a tad to the right of the way they were walking and said, "I see dust. More dust than those Blackfoot should be stirring up, even at a dead run!"

Longarm followed her gaze, nodded, and pointed out a far more distant dust haze to the southeast, saying, "Yonder go them rascals we just brushed with. That closer dust cloud would be the bigger bunch that Blackfoot warned his pals about. I'd say they were riding hard, a mite to the far side of the Bozeman Trail. Like us, they have that other dust cloud in view and they're out to ask Mister Lo to cease and desist his current mischief."

He started to swing over that way, but as quickly turned back. "They'll have ridden on by before we can hope to head 'em off, and even if we could, they've likely got more urgent chores to tend. At least we don't have to worry about those Blackfoot as we concentrate on picking 'em up and laying 'em down."

"I'm going to lash that paint pony good if ever we catch up with him!" she grumbled, trudging on at Longarm's side as the sun rose ever hotter and the slope got ever steeper.

Longarm said, "It might head back to the Price place unless it knows of fodder and water closer. We'd best worry about that once we get on into town and have something faster than our poor aching feet to get about on. I'm pretty sure my personal saddle and possibles have made it most ways to a livery down in Douglas by now. Unless someone tells 'em different, with a firm hand on the reins, ponies tend to head on home for a bite to eat."

Crow Mary, who'd never met Miss Stephanie Chandler of the *Baltimore Herald*, naturally wanted to hear more about his missing McClellan and livery mount. So he told her. Conversation helped them pass the time, and it sure was taking them some time to get anywhere today.

The sun was almost straight overhead in a hot blue bowl of cloudless sky by the time they'd wearied of all the trouble Stephanie might or might not have gotten into. It had been obvious to begin with, to both of them, that the Eastern girl holding the horses for him had bolted in panic when she'd lost sight of him near that night fire in the spooky darkness. As a big gray prairie locust buzzed like a rattler and flew up from the grass right in front of them on mock butterfly wings, the Indian girl added, "That wooded draw I told you about lies just over that next rise, and it's going to get a lot hotter before it gets any cooler."

Longarm strode on with her a spell, chewing an unlit cheroot and wishing it was pemmican, before he said, "I've been afoot at three in the afternoon in dry country before. If there's water as well as shade up ahead, our bellies can likely take being empty a mite longer than our brains can take baking dry."

She said there was water if you dug for it, but proposed they nibble the buds and bulbs the country offered in abundance this time of year. He said he'd eat *her* if they didn't damn it get there mighty soon. He hadn't considered how that could be taken till she laughed sort of dirty and broke into a merry dog trot, insisting, "Let's hurry, then. I can hardly wait!"

Chapter 9

In point of fact they were both too hot and sweaty to feel up to
French lessons by the time they'd run down the far slope into the
cottonwoods, chokecherries, and willows shading both banks
of a sometime prairie stream. As they reeled to a happy halt
in the astoundingly cooler shade, Longarm saw that however
deep the water might tear through these parts when there was
snow or rain on the Bighorns to the west, the sand lay flat,
wide, and dry as a two-lane post road now. But as if to make
up for that, the grass grew green between the trees to either
side, and most of the trees were in bud as well as early leaf.
The chokecherries had already blossomed and set fruit. But
bitty green chokecherries were too sour to even consider yet.
They were still pretty poor cherries when they got ripe later
on. Crow Mary plucked some milkweed buds and handed them
to him as she scouted for something better. Longarm popped
them in his mouth without asking what they were. Milkweed
sure grew funny. The sticky white juice that kids called "milk"
was bitter and could make you sick if you were stupid enough
to swallow much of it. Within a few weeks the buds he was
chewing would be balls of fluff as interesting to eat as cotton
balls. But right now, fixing to flower and set seed, they tasted
sort of like raw string beans.

The gal had long since returned his sixgun, of course, but he still swung the muzzle of his Winchester in the direction of a sudden flurry of hoofbeats. Crow Mary crabbed for cover behind a clump of willow without having to be instructed in such matters. So Longarm drew his Colt, tossed it silently to her, and motioned her to stay put as he eased on up the draw to scout those disturbing sounds.

The critter pawing the earth with its hooves sounded disturbed as well. It didn't seem to be headed anywhere in particular, even though it seemed to want to go there quickly.

Then, as Longarm eased through a willow fork to spy a paint rump and swishing tail, he had to laugh. He moved closer to make sure, and then called out, "It's your runaway paint, Miss Mary. He's snagged that long rawhide lead he was dragging on some tree roots, and that ought to learn him not to be so independent!"

He was holding the paint steady and recoiling the long braided line by the time the Indian girl got to them through the tanglewood, fussing and cussing. Longarm had already punched the paint in the muzzle a time or two to calm it down. So he told the girl not to as he took his sixgun back, saying, "We could ride on, double, or we could scout up more salad greens to nibble in this fine shade. I generally leave such choices to the lady I happen to be with."

She smiled like a mean little kid and replied, "The longer I know you, the more ladies I think you've been with. Was that Wasichu girl who rode off with your other horses a better lay than me?"

He chuckled fondly and said, "That's an unfair question in more ways than one. Even if I was inclined to kiss and tell, we both know I'm in no position to compare the two of you that way."

She looked away and took a deep breath before she spoke. "I really need that five dollars you said you might give me. Do you have that silly pony tethered good?"

He nodded. "Yep. But before we get silly ourselves, I'd best set you straight about some of my personal habits. To begin with, I ain't in the custom of paying ladies to, ah, like me."

She pouted her lower lip at him and demanded, "Why did you offer me that money then? I don't have anything but my pony and my body to sell. I've only got one pony now and, hear me, I need both a mount and some hard cash if I'm ever going to get home again!"

He tried to soothe her. "I had a ride to town, a *pony* ride to town, in mind when I mentioned money, Miss Mary. I should have known better than to mention money and then let you dangle. For I've been broke myself, and I know the feeling."

He reached in his pocket, fished out a ten-dollar gold piece, and handed it to her, saying, "Let's say this eagle covers lunch in this swell shade as well as the hire of this fool paint as far as town. Then let's say no more about it."

But she stared down surprised at the wherewithal to get her home with change left over. "Are you sure that's all you really want? What's the matter with me? I took a bath just last Saturday and washed my hands and face this very morning!"

He smiled and said, "That makes you cleaner as well as prettier than me, ma'am. There ain't nothing wrong with you. Can't we try and separate finances from friendship, or better yet, find something more solid to *eat* around here?"

She laughed and led him further up the draw to where a bed of prairie potatoes or ground nuts, as some called them, grew handy to a sward of love grass between a cottonwood and some peach willow.

He sat on the love grass in his shirtsleeves, setting aside his rifle, roll, and even his sweated-up Stetson to admire Crow Mary as she dug a mess of prairie potatoes with a barlow knife from the skin purse she wore tucked through the waistband holding her Mother Hubbard modestly in place.

Prairie potatoes were neither potatoes nor nuts, albeit they tasted something like potatoes if you cooked them, or something like nuts if you ate them raw. In point of fact they were sort of glorified grass roots that looked like chick-peas strung on frayed butcher's twine. The Indian gal cleaned them good enough to chew by swishing them through the love-grass stems.

Love grass was really grass, so called because livestock just loved hell out of it. It had just a hint of vanilla to its juicy stems if human beings cared to try it. It felt just swell to sprawl on whether you cared to nibble on it or not. So once she'd gathered a lapful of prairie potatoes, the young Indian gal stretched out on the springy sod beside Longarm and they talked some more as they ate and lazed in the dappled shade.

He tried to steer the conversation along the straight and narrow, knowing how the government he rode for felt about taking advantage of public wards. That's what they called screwing Indians, taking advantage of public wards. Longarm knew the line was drawn a tad tighter than that. Raping an Indian gal on a B.I.A. or military reserve could get a man hanged, on the rare occasions charges were pressed and made to stick. Screwing consenting adult Indians could still get a white boy in a whole lot of trouble if he messed with a gal on her own agency and the agent found out about it. The B.I.A., and lots of others who said they were out to do right by Mister Lo, seemed to feel Indians were big babies who didn't know right from wrong and needed proper guidance from the same superior race that had seven-year-old orphans working in cotton mills, coal mines, and such back East.

Indians off the reserve but not on the army's wanted list, such as this one crunching away at his side, were allowed more leeway in their relationships with whites, and vice versa. Longarm knew he could get in real trouble offering the pretty little thing a drink of trade likker. But nobody really cared if she just gave herself to whites.

He got out his pocket watch to check the time, and whistled softly when he saw how early it still was. When she asked what he might be upset about, he said, "I'm more surprised than chagrined. With all that's happened since we left the Price spread, I figured the day was almost over. But it ain't even three yet, and this cool shade in this draw is a pure illusion. I'll bet it's hot as Hell's hinges out on the open prairie now!"

She said it was getting hot enough there in the shade, and asked how he could stand those wool pants and heavy gauge shirt he had on. He shrugged and allowed that had there been a swimming hole anywhere along this draw he'd have been proud to go swimming with her in his birthday suit, but since there wasn't, he couldn't.

She unfastened her waistband, softly observing, "I'd like to go swimming with you. Since, as you say, we have no water to swim in, would you like me to show you another excuse to get undressed?"

He laughed and said, "I told you that money was just for the ride to town."

To which she demurely replied, as she slipped the Mother Hubbard off over her head, "I know. I like it better when I'm just doing it because I like somebody too."

He didn't have any answer that Billy Vail might approve. But who cared whether anyone else approved or not, once she'd sprawled on her naked back in the love grass to display all those tawny curves and enticing privates for his approval. It would have been downright rude to say anything but, "Powder River and let her buck!" as he shucked his own duds to roll aboard her. So that was what he did, and it felt interesting as well as grand. For like many Indian gals she was even more naked than expected between her wide-spread copper thighs.

There was some argument as to whether Indians were simply lacking in body hair or inclined to pluck such hairs as they began to sprout in early puberty. He didn't think this was the time or place to ask. She locked her high-buttons around his naked waist and commenced to pant in his face like a pup as he pounded her. He knew she considered that more romantic than kissing. So he panted back. It was just as easy and no sillier than spit-swapping when one studied on it. But she'd picked up enough Wasichu notions to reach up and grab him by the hair to reel him in for some home-style kissing, assuming one's home was in France, as they climaxed together in an easy home-style way.

They did it again, with her thighs spread wider and her brown behind clean off the grass, once he had a knee of hers hooked over each of his stiff-armed elbows so he could really get to moving in her. Then they shared a cheroot to cool their love-slicked flesh and get their second winds. When she said she wanted to get on top, Longarm told her to hold her horses while he made sure the one pony they had left was all right.

It was. It neighed and fought that rawhide lead as if it had never seen a naked white man wearing a gun rig and packing a knife before.

As Longarm busted off a cottonwood limb and trimmed the splintery end with the whittle-blade of his jackknife he said soothingly, "I know how juicy them leaves you've been brousing are this time of year, Paint. We'd still best put some real water in you before you have to carry two grownups the rest of the way into town."

As he dug nearby in the soft sand he went on, "Your warm-natured owner and me won't be leaving this cool shade till the sun sinks lower over the Bighorns, way over yonder. But once we do ask you to pack us, we'll expect you to get us there in time for an early supper. Prairie potatoes are better than nothing, but they don't stick to the ribs worth mention."

The sand was moist less than six inches down. He scooped a broader than deeper basin about a yard and a half across and, sure enough, it commenced to fill with sand-filtered water about as clear and likely as safe to drink as fresh piss.

The paint pony seemed to think it was swell. Longarm tossed his digging stick aside, patted the paint's rump, and went back to where he'd left Crow Mary, pulling up more roots.

She'd found a couple of Indian turnips to go with the juicy but sort of insipid prairie potatoes. They weren't really turnips, of course, but their radishy tang made them almost worth the chewing.

He naturally got to considering even tangier pleasures, now that he had his second wind. But when he snubbed out the last of their smoke and reached for some ass, the previously friendly Indian rolled away to lay on her naked belly and breasts, all teary-eyed and fussing at him in her own lingo.

He started to ask for a translation. Then he wondered why any man who'd ever been fussed at by women at times like this would want to put himself through that same old shit in English. So he sat up and plucked a grass stem to chew. Neither tobacco nor emergency rations did a whole lot for a man who was trying to remember exactly what an apple pie washed down with real Arbuckle coffee tasted like—after, say, a steak and real potatoes mashed and buttered.

After an all-too-short while the Indian gal sniffed and asked him if he didn't want to know what she was so upset about. He suspected he knew, but it was only polite to ask. So he did, and wasn't all that surprised to hear her pout, "I think you were only having fun with me. If I'd been a Wasichu girl you would have treated me with more respect. You think all Absaroke girls are whores now."

82

"Not all," he said, truthfully enough. It would have been impolite to point out it had been her notion to offer more than a pony ride for that eagle he'd slipped her. So he said, "You didn't do anything just now that *I* wasn't willing to do. It ain't true that I wouldn't have wanted to do it if you'd been, let's say, a pink-eyed blonde. I screwed an albino gal one time. She was traveling with a freak show for some reason. I told her the same thing I'm telling you. A pretty gal is a pretty gal no matter how light or dark her hide and hair might be. But I'll take back what we just done if you like, and we'll just get dressed and say it never happened, hear?"

She laughed, wiping at her face with the back of her hand, and told him not to be silly, adding, "I want you again. I deserve to be beaten, beaten like a wild unruly pony."

He was pretty certain she'd never been beaten as a naughty girl-child. Few Indians smacked their kids for doing what came naturally. It was likely the asshole missionaries who'd sprinkled her that they could thank for all this bullshit on an otherwise grand occasion.

He tried again. "Well, I want you some more too. So what do you figure we ought to do about it, get dressed and apologize or let you get on top like you asked before?"

She sobbed that they were all going to burn in Hell with the other lost souls, red and white, even as she rolled him on his back to fork a brown thigh across him. Finding she'd caught him by surprise down there, she took the matter firmly in hand, assuring him, "This is not what I want to do. Hear me, I am possessed by Okihadi, the spirit you call the Evil One!"

He didn't feel up to arguing theology as she got it up for him again. But once she had, and they'd come together again, he rolled her on her own back to let it sort of soak in her as he murmured, in a conversational tone, "Them Blackfoot would call you Okihadi the Wendigo, and that reminds me. Your kind and mine have had misunderstandings in the past inspired by religious fanatics, red as well as white. You've heard about them Paiute prophets and their odd notions about medicine shirts and ghost dancing?"

She raised her knees to cushion his hips even more nicely with her soft haunches as she wrinkled her pert nose and said, "Not *my* people. We don't like to see ghosts. Those Heyoka promises to wake all the dead of all the nations so they can all run around at once sounds like a very bad idea. Where would that many people find enough to eat, even if there was room to pitch that many lodges?"

He smiled thinly at the picture and confided, "I thought I'd thrashed that out with your Lakota cousins the time I dealt with some ghost dancers a spell back. The point of all this otherwise idle speculation is that some Lakota are still searching for some answers and, seeing they just can't lick the U.S. Cav, they've gotten mighty mystical of late."

She purred, "Move it in me some more. Why are we talking about troublemaking Heyoka chanters driving stupid Lakota *witco*? When they tried to stir up trouble on *our* reserve our own dream singers drove them away with pony quirts. Nobody can make a buckskin shirt stop bullets just by painting medicine signs on it, even if they are not the medicine sighs of another nation. If the Paiute know how to turn away bullets, how come everyone else has always picked on them?"

He found himself moving in her sweet warm wetness again as he sighed and said, "I hope we convinced them Blackfoot they weren't bullet proof this morning. I sure wish they'd been Lakota, Cheyenne, or even Shoshone, though. For I can buy some troublemaker acting up on a reserve within riding distance better than I can buy that troublemaker riding all the way down from northern Montana for no sensible . . . Never mind what I said and let's do this right!"

They did but, being a woman, Crow Mary naturally wanted him to tell her what he'd told her not to mind. So he explained, "It makes no sense to ascribe sensible motives to Indians acting wild by definition, no offense. Half the trouble betwixt your kind and mine has been caused by one side of the other trying to figure what in blue blazes the other could be thinking of, and then thinking up the wrong answer."

She frowned and said, "Hear me, my kind has not been at war with your kind since Liver Eating Johnson made peace with all Absaroke in the Shining Times of the beaver trade."

He patted her bare ass reassuringly and said, "I know how friendly you are, Miss Mary. But riders inspired by *witco* religious notions can go to a whole heap of trouble a more sensible rider might not see fit to. Back on the other side of the great bitter water, where my kind started out, a whole bunch of boys in tin pants mounted up and rode farther than from here to, say, Boston just to get at some other old boys who wore towels on their fool heads. A dream singer called Peter the Hermit convinced 'em they'd all live forever in the lodge of the Great Spirit if only they'd paint red crosses on their shirts and ride clean off the map after Heathen Turks and the Holy Grail."

She asked what that had to do with those damned Blackfoot who'd killed her buckskin and scared her half to death. So he saw he was talking more to himself than anyone else and replied, "Just trying to decide how far a fool might ride for superstitious notions. I got to catch one before I can ask him what in thunder he thinks he might be after. Meanwhile, the shadows are commencing to lengthen a mite. We ought to start thinking about getting on into Pumpkin Buttes some time this side of sundown."

She said, "We have time to do it some more. Then I think we ought to slip into town one at a time from two directions. If they see us ride in together on one pony they will know we did it."

He felt no call to argue. She was right. Town loafers never missed the chance to call a luckier cuss a squaw man, and Crow Mary was the sort of squaw they thought about, jerking off out back when they had no strangers, male or female, to smirk at.

He said, "Well, I do have to send me some telegrams and then hang about for some answers once we get to town. Where do you suggest we meet up in Pumpkin Buttes after dark?"

She looked away and softly said, "I don't think we ought to meet this way again at all. I have nothing to keep me in that Wasichu town, nothing. I think I should buy the few things I need for the long ride home, and then I think I should just ride on, in the dark, and put some distance between me and those Blackfoot before I make camp again in some place like this one. Don't you think I am right?"

He was so relieved by her sensible attitude that he could have kissed her. So he did and, as long as they were at it, put it to her dog-style while he still had the chance.

85

Chapter 10

Once a trail town such as Pumpkin Buttes got started along one fool trail or another, it tended to collect cross trails, telegraph lines, railroad spurs, and such. Since hardly any way in or out of Pumpkin Buttes was in heavy use because of the Indian scare, Crow Mary was able to drop Longarm off within an easy walk without them attracting any suspicious glances. She said she'd just sit her paint behind that screen of tall sunflower shoots just off the Western Union service trail and let him follow the poles a spell before she cut over to the railroad tracks and followed *them* into town, knowing hardly anyone would be waiting for any trains that just weren't running this evening.

As he gave her sweet round rump a parting pat and slid off the Indian side of the Indian pony with his Winchester and rolled tweeds, he felt obliged to intimate they might meet up again as friendly, Lord willing and neither of 'em came down with anything fatal. She knew how the game of love was played by grown lovers too. So she said she'd be looking forward to it, freeing him to just start walking, not looking back. He figured he'd have enough trouble forgetting her before he ever again got as close to anything as good-natured and grand.

They'd made good time from that shady nest in the draw, but since they'd had such a swell time there, it was later in the day than it really needed to be. He saw tar-paper roofing and tin chimneys just above the next grassy rise, and paused by a sun-silvered telegraph pole to unroll his coat and vest so he could stroll into town properly dressed for suppertime. A heap of folks seemed to notice him anyway as he strode in out of nowhere just before sundown with a Winchester cradled in the crook of one arm and a cross-draw Colt riding the opposite hip under his open-for-any-business frock coat. But nobody had anything to say as Longarm passed, so he just kept passing till he found the black and yellow sign of the telegraph office near the railroad siding and strode on in.

The buck-toothed and four-eyed young galoot riding for Western Union in these parts said the wires were still up, as far as he could tell, but that no, there were no messages for any U.S. Deputy Custis Long. So Longarm got cracking with a pencil and some yellow Western Union blanks to dispatch messages and inquiries north, south, east, and west, charging the nickel-a-word day rates to his home office. When the neighborly clerk pointed out it was almost night, and that night-letter rates were cheaper, Longarm replied, "Thanks just the same but I want 'em sent direct in hopes of early replies, for as you'll notice whilst you're sending 'em, I've come a long way and done wonders without knowing shit about what's going on up this way!"

The clerk nodded soberly and said, "I see you've writ Blackfoot on this top telegram form. Were you with that big posse as rid out after Blackfoot earlier today?"

Longarm shook his head. "Might have seen their dust. Know I saw some Blackfoot. Feel free to read all about it as you get them messages off to all concerned. I'll come back later this evening, and by then mayhaps we'll both know more about it, like the old song promises."

The clerk asked what song they might be jawing about. Longarm said he'd likely be at the nearest saloon, after some supper and a courtesy call on the local law, if anything really urgent came in before he got back. Then he offered the clerk a cheroot, lit it for himself when the kid said he prefered to chew, and stepped back out in the balmly orange-to-purple gloaming, pausing on the plank steps long enough to get his bearings as if he'd really know where in thunder he was.

Seeing he didn't, he stepped back to the doorway to call in, "I see no indications out here as to where you folk keep your greasy spoons or pewter badges."

The clerk called back, "There's a chop-suey joint just around the next corner, north. Ain't no official law in town. Such trouble as we have is handled by a Converse County deputy called Larkin. He's mostly out to his cattle spread, the Slash L, up the Bozeman a ways. You won't find him there now, though. Old Larkin rid out with them other Indian hunters I just mentioned."

Longarm smiled thinly. "Bueno. I felt more hungry than polite to begin with. If there ain't no town law I have to pay my respects to, I'd best go make friends with some chop suey, or better yet, some of them foolish young eggs."

He turned away a second time to stride north along the plank walk with more purpose, softly singing to himself.

> Farther along, we'll know more about it.
> Farther along, we'll understand why.
> Cheer up, my brother, walk in the sunshine.
> We'll understand it, all, by and by.

That clerk was likely a Papist if he'd never heard the sort of optimistic old Calvinist hymn, Longarm decided. He had his doubts about its promise himself. Many things happened that were never fully understood.

Longarm remembered the strange case of Kasper Hauser. He'd read about it, and was sure glad the U.S. Justice Department didn't have to worry about that poor German kid who'd wandered into the Nuremberg Police Station out of nowhere with a mighty wild tale of being raised in the dark by mysterious lunatics. Then he'd gotten stabbed to death, by a person or persons unknown, just about the time the poor German lawmen had him figured for a lying halfwit.

There were heaps of things nobody was ever likely to know more about, let alone *all* about. He was certain now that some sort of Indians were acting mighty odd in these parts, and at least two independent witnesses who could have known had identified them as Blackfoot. But after that, Longarm reserved the right to change his mind the moment he had evidence to the contrary. That dyed moccasin had read Blackfoot to him as well. But that one shield cover had been Pawnee, and he'd buy a Blackfoot bragging with Lakota feather signs as soon as he got a paid-up member of the Siksika Nation to explain what those infernal ermine tails they often wore stood for if they didn't stand for enemies mistreated in various interesting ways.

He found the Chinese restaurant where the Western Union clerk had said he might. But the bitty hole-in-the-wall seemed to be shuttered against the night, even though the evening sky still glowed bright enough to read by. As he stood there searching for some words of explanation to read, an amiable-looking townie with a drinker's nose informed him, "Ain't no use looking for any of the smaller joints to be open, stranger. With Deputy Larkin and his pals out after Indians, the Chinee, Mexicans, and such are doubtless hiding under their beds in hopes of surviving till Larkin gets back."

Longarm frowned thoughtfully. "I got to eat supper if I mean to survive my ownself. Who or what's got everyone so scared with your law out chasing Indians?"

The townie replied, "Not everyone. Just poor bastards with no white pals to back their play, should Woolly Bob Waterman and his boys get to upholding the honor of Southern womankind again. You might be able to get something to eat at the Elkhorn Saloon, up Main Street a piece. If you go there, though, remember you rid for Texas whether you did or not. Just saying you was for the South ain't good enough when Woolly Bob has his Rebel flag waving."

Longarm didn't ask further details about Woolly Bob. He was just too hungry to care. There was always a town bully, inclined to act up when the town law wasn't looking. Longarm had no use for bullies. But he hadn't worried about them all that much since he'd been a mighty small boy. So he thanked his informant for the doubtless good advice and retraced his steps to Main Street, from whence it was easy enough to find the Elkhorn in the gathering dusk. There were more than a dozen cow ponies tethered out front, and if that hadn't indicated some evening activity in town, an out-of-tune piano was playing "Green Grow the Lilacs," loud as possible with the foot pedal down as far as it would go.

So nobody was facing the batwings of the doorway as Longarm parted them to sashay in. The crowd of about two dozen men and three or four soiled doves in bright sateen that could have used some dry cleaning were all facing the piano against the back wall, where a husky cuss wearing woolly chaps, an old Confederate cavalry hat, and a brace of Walker conversions was facing them in return, singing the old Texican hymn, or march, in the dulcet tones of a tone-deaf coyote. Nobody but a Mex singer or maybe a castrated Irish tenor could hope to hit such high notes right, even if they'd been in the song. But Longarm managed not to laugh at the poor singing fool as he moseyed his way to one end of the bar, rested his Winchester in the resultant corner, and ordered a Maryland rye with a draft chaser.

He didn't drink that seriously on an empty stomach as a rule. But he didn't want anyone making unkind comments when he got at that free lunch tray he'd already spotted further down and, right now, out of easy reach.

He waited till he'd been served, and snapped a silver dollar down on the mock mahogany, before he asked if those were really deviled eggs and pickled pigs' feet down yonder.

The heavy-set Hibernian type tending bar replied, not unkindly, "We got potato salad and mousetrap cheese as well. But it's only fair to warn you Woolly Bob Waterman likes everything on the tray but the pickled pigs' feet. That's him singing, and he rode in just now with four other boys off the E-X-E spread."

Longarm sipped some suds, leaving the rye untasted till he had a safer place to put it, and muttered, "I heard your town bully was in town. Are you saying you're afraid to slide them eats meant for paying customers to a paying customer?"

The barkeep scowled and growled, "Where would they go to drink if they ran *me* out of town? It's your funeral if you're too hungry to listen to your elders, buck."

Nobody but the hulking brute singing falsetto by the piano seemed to notice as the barkeep moved down to the tray and carried it on up to Longarm's end. Woolly Bob kept on singing, if that was why he was making all those awful noises. So Longarm started with a deviled egg wrapped in mousetrap cheese, and once he'd washed that down with beer and dug into the potato salad, he felt it was safe to sip some of that harder liquor, and wonder of wonders, it was really Maryland rye. So he felt good enough to join in the applause when the asshole by the piano ran out of things to sing about lilacs and had to stop.

Someone else was singing much better, about the mocking bird that sang on Sweet Hattie's grave, and Longarm was helping himself to more potato salad when he heard a grumble close to his ear, deep as a lovesick buffalo with a belly ache. "They tell me you were told not to eat nothing on that tray but the pigs' feet, pilgrim!"

Longarm got his back to the otherwise empty corner so he could see the innocent-eyed barkeep wiping up imaginary spills, way off in the distance, and verify that Woolly Bob was really capable of growling so deep in his burly chest when he wasn't singing in a more sissified way.

Longarm swallowed the mouthful of free lunch the asshole seemed to want to argue about and replied, in a firm, friendly tone, "If you were most anyone else, I'd point out there's still enough on the tray to feed a family of average eaters. Since I know you laid claim to the hog's share in hopes of provoking a fight, feel free to fill your fist anytime you desire to die, you poor brainless piss-ant."

The local bully blanched. Longarm had meant him to. Longarm hadn't raised his voice above a conversational level. But others in the smoke-filled saloon had been expecting a show. As Woolly Bob laughed uneasily and yelled, "Great day in the morning, it's Wild Bill Hickock returned from the grave to spank us all and send us to bed without no suppers!" he suddenly seemed to sprout a pair of armed and dangerous-looking galoots to either side of him.

Nobody else in the Elkhorn seemed to want any part of the action. As the five roughly dressed and hard-eyed riders were given plenty of elbow room to deal with one lone stranger, a squint-eyed cuss to their leader's right asked, in an amused tone, whether old Bob was sure it was old Wild Bill and not Calamity Jane. "He's dressed too pretty to piss standing up, Woolly Bob. What's he done to offend us so?"

The boss bully smiled crookedly at Longarm as he explained, "I only asked if he meant to hog all them eats, and the next thing I knowed he was offering to duel me to the death."

When Squint Eye asked Longarm whether he was drunk or *loco en la cabeza,* their intended victim simply smiled wolfishly and replied, "If I was looking for kid fights I'd hang around school yards more often. When an asshole wearing guns starts up with another man wearing a gun, he'd best be serious about fighting. I know *I* am, and since any number can play, it's only fair to warn you I pack five in the wheel of the weapon you see and a couple more in one I'll be hauling out later, if any of you sons of bitches are still on your feet by the time I've fired my first five shots."

Woolly Bob actually took a backward step before he remembered his local rep, took a deep breath, and soberly declared, "That's quite a brag, considering what we'd be doing in the meantime, pilgrim. Do you really think you could get off that many shots, well aimed, with me and my boys returning every compliment?"

Longarm shrugged and replied, "Your point's well took. I'd likely go down too in a five-to-one shootout. But looking on the bright side, I'd likely take at least half of you with me, starting with the first mother who slaps leather, and I don't mean Mother Nature. So I reckon I'm ready whenever you are, Woolly Bob."

The object of his ominous affection, like most full-grown bullies, had managed to grow all that way up by crawfishing when he figured it was crawfish time. So grasping the straw Longarm had held out by addressing him by name, Woolly Bob laughed mockingly and said, "Oh, now I got the measure of this apparent lunatic. He ain't out to fight us for the free lunch, boys. He's a hired gun, out to settle what certain parties dasn't try to prove in court."

"You mean Ross Larkin sent for this mean-talking cuss, to take on the five of us *alone*?" asked a hitherto-silent side-kick.

To which Woolly Bob replied in a knowing tone, "Whether he's alone or just baiting us is neither here nor there. Add it up and it only reads one way. Ross Larkin all but accuses us right out of running his damn brand. Then he gathers almost all the men in town to ride out on some wild-goose chase, leaving us at the mercy of this unknown quality who's been spoiling for a shootout since I first laid eyes on him and vice versa."

The one with the squint stared hard at Longarm to opine, "He don't look good enough to me. No one man is good enough if you want to say the word, Woolly Bob."

But Woolly Bob must not have wanted to say the word. Not any fighting word, at any rate. He nodded soberly at Longarm and said, "Eat the whole tray and tell Larkin I'd rather have it out in court, the way I told him to begin with. Seems to me a man so sure he'd send away for the likes of you would have something better to back his wild words. For Gawd's sake, he's supposed to be a lawman, part-time leastways. Ain't Larkin never heard of ever-dense?"

Longarm repressed a smile and said, "I think evidence is the word you're groping for, Woolly Bob. What has the town law been accusing you of? Aside from being a general pain in the ass, I mean."

Squint Eye sneered, "Don't act innocent, gunslick. Larkin would hardly hire outside help without mentioning that bullshit about stray stock and the ease of running his Slash L to our E-X-E."

But before Longarm could get more than that out of them, Woolly Bob snapped, "*Vamanos, muchachos!* Can't you see he's trying to steer the talk into dangerous waters in front of a saloon full of witnesses?"

They must have agreed. For the next thing Longarm knew he seemed to have that end of the bar and the free lunch atop it all to his lonesome. As he heard them riding off, outside, the barkeep grabbed his beer schooner to put a fresh head on his beer for free, saying, "All right, you didn't listen to your elders and for that we thank you. I was sure you were done for, though. How did you get to be so tough, Mister, ah . . . ?"

"Just call me Custis, for now," replied Longarm. "I'm still a mite confused about the conversation I just had. Am I to believe your local law and aspiring cattle baron has accused those boys of running his brand and then let them run *loose*?"

The barkeep said, "It ain't that cut and dried. What a man missing stock can prove and what an artist with a running iron might be doing to his brand are two debates entire. It don't take a genius to see how easy it would be to run Larkin's brand to an E-X-E. But after that things get more confounding."

Longarm asked how. So the older man, who knew local gossip in more detail confided, "To begin with, Ross Larkin ain't the only stockman whose stock has wound up lost, strayed, or stolen. Larkin's lost way fewer head than some, and other cows, a heap of other cows, wore brands that just can't be run to an E-X-E."

Longarm sipped his rye soberly. "In other words, the cow thieves have been driving 'em off their home range entire, likely to be sold at another railhead."

The barkeep nodded. "The stealing's stopped since them Indians started raiding and the railroads stopped running. But whether Woolly Bob and his pals are honest or not when the trains are running, the fact remains they don't own the E-X-E. They just run it for an Eastern owner, a widow woman who lives in Boston Town, I hear. So why would a handful of hired hands and a not-too-bright foreman like old Woolly Bob be changing Ross Larkin's brand, or anyone's brand, to that of a herd they don't own and couldn't sell if they got away with such a dumb and obvious stunt?"

Longarm finished his rye. "Well, I can see how a man missing stock could leap to dumb conclusions about dumb neighbors. But most cow thieves I've met tend to get in fewer pointless fights."

The barkeep agreed and cautiously added, "You never said what point you had in mind when you stood up to the five of 'em. I don't recall you saying whether they was right or wrong in assuming you to be an, ah . . . range detective?"

"That's a polite way to describe a hired gun," said Longarm, not really saying all that much. Then he picked up his Winchester and simply turned away from the barkeep and that silver dollar on the bar with no further comment. For the nosey cuss had struck him as just a mite two-faced, and while the salty so-called free lunch had dulled his appetite considerably a man would be a fool to really fill up on such heavy grub before bedtime, even if he knew where in thunder he was going to bed down in this fool town.

He went back to the telegraph office to jaw some more with the less sneaky-looking clerk. The only reply to any of his earlier messages, so far, had just come in from Douglas. Miss Stephanie Chandler of the *Baltimore Herald* had indeed made it back to the nearest active railroad stop alive, and had barely stopped in her headlong flight from the Savage Blackfoot, to hear her tell it. The four ponies had kept company with her, as he'd hoped, at least as far as their own livery stalls. So they were pleased to learn Longarm was still alive after all, and said his McClellan, spare socks, and such would be waiting for him in the tack room of the Douglas Livery if ever he tired of chasing Savage Blackfoot on foot.

Longarm chuckled when he got to that part, and turning to the bucktoothed clerk, said, "I'd save time hiring another horse and saddle hereabouts instead of strolling all the way back to Douglas on my already weary hind legs. So I'd be much obliged if you could steer me to a closer livery, and while you're about it, I could sure use the address of a good cheap hotel too."

The clerk asked how long he meant to stay in Pumpkin Buttes. So Longarm truthfully replied he didn't know, explaining, "I got to wait on answers to them wires I sent out earlier. Once my boss, Marshal Vail, gets that report confirming real Indians really killing folks, he's likely to order me on back to Denver. There's times we can handle things delicate for the B.I.A., and there's times the U.S. Cav has its chores cut out for it. What's all that got to do with finding me a flop for the night?"

The clerk said, "There isn't any regular hotel in Pumpkin Buttes, good or bad at any price. But I board with the Widow Stern, who just so happens to run the second largest livery in these parts. She got to be a widow when her husband thought he could ride a known man-killer and found out he couldn't. It was a closed-casket ceremony, the summer before last."

Longarm nodded soberly and said, "I'd be obliged if you could steer me to this Stern widow who deals in bed, board, and broncos. I take it they've long since shot the bronc as killed her man?"

To which the clerk replied, "Hell, no. She busted the brute herself, and sold him for more than enough to pay for her husband's funeral."

Chapter 11

Longarm was expecting a stern lady indeed. So when he got to the three-story boarding house across the corral from the Stern Livery, he was inclined to take the pretty little thing who came to the front door for a daughter of the house. But when he asked the petite blonde whether he might have a word with Widow Stern, she dimpled up at him to confide, "You'd be talking to her. I'm Elsa Stern. So who might you be and what might I be doing for you at this hour?"

He produced his badge and identification as he apologized for pestering her so late in the evening. When he added he was in the market for at least bed and breakfast, along with the hire of two ponies with a pack and stock saddle as well, she told him to come right into her parlor and have some cake and coffee.

He followed her, noting with approval that the place smelled of lemon oil and a recently baked chocolate cake. There were two older gents and a young mousy female boarder in the parlor for the more spectacular widow to introduce him to before he got to sit down on a window seat near her rolltop corner desk. She rang for her kitchen help with a handy bell pull on the far side of her desk as she sat her own shapely self in a chair and asked if Longarm would like to talk first about broncs or breakfast.

He said he'd eat most anything that didn't snap back. So they were jawing about the ponies he'd need after that when a pretty colored gal came in with coffee and cake for everyone in the room.

Skinny Miss Olivier, if he had her name right, allowed the widow was out to spoil both her and her figure with these late-night treats. But she helped herself to a healthy slice anyway. Longarm saw why as soon as he dug in. When he said it was the best chocolate cake he'd tasted this side of a fancy Chicago bakery, he expected the young widow to accept the compliment whether she deserved it or not. But old Elsa nodded at her colored help and said, "Jasmine here baked it. Wait till you taste her buckwheat cakes in the morning."

One of the other male boarders, named Smithers or something, opined Jasmine's waffles were even better and that nobody scrambled eggs half as fine. The young colored gal looked as if she might be blushing. It was tough to tell. She was pretty dark for a gal with such white features. As she turned away to dash back to her kitchen, Longarm noticed she had the same-shaped ass as an Irish gal he knew back in Denver.

Knowing it was dumb to study the hired help of any hostess that way, Longarm washed down the cake in his mouth and left the rest on his plate till they'd settled on two bits a day per pony, with the gear thrown in. She said, "You may want to see if you can get a better price from the Ace Corral if you think I'm holding you up because of this Indian scare. Whether you believe me or not, I charge the same in good times or bad. Saves a heap of bookkeeping."

He said he found her prices fair, considering how far they were from all that much competition. He managed not to comment when she said his bed and breakfast was going to cost him a flat buck. It was small wonder she could afford to keep her place so clean and comfortable. It wouldn't have been polite to ask what her other guests paid by the week, with them sitting there. He didn't see how either old gent or the mousy Miss Olivier could afford thirty damned dollars a month no matter how much extra coffee and cake old Jasmine served. The poor skinny drab with spiderweb-colored hair was some sort of sales-clerk at a Main Street notions shop, if he'd heard her right.

Before he could ask her again, Miss Olivier allowed it was getting late and that she'd drop off her own cup and saucers on her way past the kitchen door. The two old coots seemed to have nothing better to do as Longarm and the young widow worked out the finances and polished off the last of that cake. Then she rose to lead him on out and up to his funny little room on the third floor.

The soft but narrow brass bedstead stood in the center of the bitty round room. He'd noticed the Carpenter's Gothic tower built up on one corner of the house as he'd come in from the street. A washstand and wardrobe stood across from one another between the arched windows cut through the curved walls. He'd have had a tougher time determining all this if a wall lamp hadn't been burning just outside in the hallway. The town of Pumpkin Buttes didn't have any street lamps lit in these parts, and the moon hadn't risen yet, if it meant to at all. The night sky was sort of overcast. His landlady pointed at an unlit candlestick on the washstand and said, "I'd be obliged if you put out all candle flames and smokes before you went to sleep. The facilities are down at the far end of the hall, should the need arise. Is there anything else you can think of that I might do for you?"

He doubted she meant that the way it could be taken. So he said there wasn't, and they shook on that and parted friendly. When she shut the door after her he saw why she'd mentioned that candle. He didn't light it, though. There were no shades in any of the windows all around, and many a man who'd back away from a face-to-face shootout might feel less shy about potshots from a safer distance.

So Longarm leaned his Winchester against the wardrobe and got undressed in the dark to hang most of his duds inside it as, way off across the rooftops, the otherwise black sky was chalk-marked now and again by distant, silent lighting. He figured it was doubtless coming down fire and salt over in the Bighorns to the west. Whether the storm swept this far east across the High Plains or not, that love nest he'd shared with Crow Mary in that wooded draw figured to be full of running water come morning. He was sorry he'd thought of that by the time he moved back to the bed with his sixgun and derringer, otherwise bare-ass. For it seemed a hell of a

98

waste to slip between clean sheets with nothing but a raging erection for company.

As he hung his cross-draw rig over a bedpost and tucked the last-ditch derringer under the edge of the mattress, he wondered if that pretty and passionate Indian gal was thinking of him right now. He told himself not to wonder. He doubted jerking off would really drive anyone totally insane, but he still preferred to save his ammunition for real prizes, and damn, that Elsa Stern was sure a pretty little thing, and doubtless a hell of a rider as well if that story about her and that man-killing bronc was true.

He fluffed the pillows and planted his busy head on them to study on more sensible matters. It helped when, a few minutes later, he heard the distant pounding of many a hoof. It sounded like a whole troop of cavalry, coming in from the south. He didn't get up to see if he could make anything out from up there. He knew that if they reined in to disband near the Elkhorn on Main Street, he wouldn't be able to. He thought about getting back up, hauling on his damned duds, and drifting over to find out if they'd found out anything. He decided it could wait. Any sign they'd cut would doubtless make more sense in the cold gray dawn, after they'd had time to calm down and he'd had time to get some answers to all those wires he'd sent out earlier.

He found himself yawning as he thought about cold gray dawns. He yawned once again for luck and closed his eyes.

That was when he heard his door opening.

He had his sixgun out and trained on the dim movement in the darkness before it occurred to him that anyone capable of opening a locked door so slick had to have done so with a key. He noticed she'd snuffed out the hall light behind her as well. He still thought he ought to ask what he could do for her, even though he knew as soon as he heard her slipping out of her night shift, whispering, "Hush! They might hear us!"

He didn't want that to happen, of course. So he just shoved his sixgun back in its holster and welcomed her with naked open arms as she slid between the covers with him, naked as a jay.

When he kissed her she kissed back, hard enough to make that tale about mastering tough ponies sound convincing. But as he ran his free hand down her squirming cuddles to warm her up, she protested, "Don't tease me! Do it! I've been dying for you to rape me since before we ever met, you good-looking moose!"

So seeing she felt that way about it, he just rolled aboard and shoved his old organ-grinder where it seemed only right, albeit who was raping whom around there seemed moot, even before she proceeded to buck and sunfish under him in a manner hinting at some deprivation as well as considerable practice. He could tell from her steam-kettle hisses and enthusiastic gushing where they were grinding that she wasn't just being polite when she softly moaned, "Oh, Lord, I'm coming already and I wanted to make it last!"

He assured her there'd be more where that come came from as he braced his bare feet against the brass foot rails and spread her thighs wider to long-dong the two of them to greater glory. As he ejaculated deep inside her firm perfumed innards, he allowed himself to imagine her blond Germanic charms contrasted with those of the dusky Crow Mary, and sure enough, that did seem to be the best cure for having to leave the Indian gal just as the party was starting to get interesting. The one they were having right now was neither better nor worse. For nine out of ten women were bodacious in bed, and the tenth was worth taking to bed as a novelty.

He didn't have to worry about that with this one. She wriggled and giggled and moaned in a mighty exciting way. But then, just as he was about to ask if she'd like to get on top so he could fight for his second wind, she suddenly whispered, "Let me up. I have to get back to my own bed, alas."

He left it right where it was, demanding, "How come? We've barely commenced, and I don't hear nobody at the door, you shy little thing."

She shoved at his naked chest more firmly with her bare palms as she pleaded, "Please take it out while I still have the strength to go! You've no idea how hard it is to protect one's reputation in a town as small as this one!"

As a matter of fact, he did. So even though he figured they were safe enough from gossip for now, he gallantly rolled off to let her rise, which she did with a speed suggesting she'd protected her reputation a heap in the past. For as ably as he could judge by blurry movement and swishy sounds in the dark, she was up and out of there before she'd slipped her night shift all the way back on.

As he lay there grinning and still tingling, he decided he was cured of any leftover longings for old Crow Mary. He hadn't gotten near enough of old Elsa Stern.

If that had been *her* just now.

As a lawman Longarm had learned not to leap to hasty conclusions, and so, even as he wiped his throbbing privates off with one corner of the top sheet, he tried to recall anything his latest conquest had said or done to indicate she was in fact the lady of the house, rather than another paying guest or, just as likely, the hired help!

He muttered, "Damn, all three were fairly young and healthy-looking, and who's to say what a particular tit or better might or might not feel like excited in the dark? I was picturing her as a beautiful blonde because that was the one I wanted most, not because she said who she *was*, before or after!"

It was a good thing he was in bed alone, he figured, as he lay there laughing like a jackass, stiff as a poker, while he pictured the blond Elsa, the dusky Jasmine, and the mousy but not badly built Miss Olivier in turn, all mighty undignified.

From a Turkish point of view, he wasn't too certain he wanted to know for certain. For as of now, it sort of felt as if he'd had all three of them, and he doubted anyone who hadn't really been there could have screwed so fine.

Chapter 12

He'd have likely found out had he been able to stay at least another night. But at breakfast the next morning neither their blond landlady at the head of the table nor Miss Olivier across from him let on they'd had any lately, and to complicate matters further there were two other female guests he hadn't met earlier, as far as he could say for certain. And the shapely Jasmine remained an unknown element, serving her fine flapjacks as if butter wouldn't melt in her mouth.

He had the chance to be alone with the pretty young widow when she led him across the corral to pick out the two ponies they'd been talking about very sedately the night before. Longarm figured it was up to the lady how or even whether she recognized a gent in public. So he kept his hands to himself and his tone platonic as she had her stable hands run out four head of riding stock for Longarm to look over.

He allowed they all seemed handsome horseflesh, and then, since he only had use for two, no matter how broad the choice, he chose a pair of bay geldings, both a hand taller than your average cow pony, and one wearing the brand of the army remount service canceled by an extra S to indicated "Sold."

She told him he's just shown her he knew how to fix himself up with a good ride. The way she smiled as she said that could

102

have been taken more ways than one. He decided it was safer to dicker for the harness he'd need to carry him and his supplies on up the Bozeman Trail.

Then he decided he'd best make certain he'd be going up it before he spent any more *dinero* on galvanized beans. So having settled with Elsa Stern, as far as he could figure, he mounted the old army pony and led the bay wearing the empty pack saddle over to the Western Union office.

There was another clerk on duty, an older gent with a walrus mustache and a more civilized approach. He'd been told to expect Longarm, and seemed impressed as he handed over a sheaf of lemon yellow envelopes, saying, "You sure kept us busy on the wire this morning, Deputy Long."

Longarm observed he'd lingered over breakfast and some other chores with that hope in mind. He offered the friendly clerk a smoke, lit his own as well, and strode back out to sit on the wooden steps as he tore the envelopes open, one by one, to see if anyone else had any notion what was going on, damn it.

The Pinkerton Detective Agency and the State of Colorado confirmed that that had really been Little Dicky and Big Dave Plimmons fixing to rob the northbound when they'd been spotted and shot instead. The Pinkertons said that the railroad dick Longarm had met up with had a good rep as well as some seniority with the company. Colorado didn't seem to care who shot train robbers as long as they did it right. Longarm wrote all the names in his notebook anyway. The railroad dick's handle was doubtless really Hamish MacNutt. Nobody would want to make up a name like that for himself. Longarm didn't see how the demise of half-ass train robbers could tie in with Indian troubles in any case, whether the Plimmons brothers had been breeds or just bragging. They were supposed to have been part Arapaho, not Blackfoot.

His Blackfoot or Siksika pal, Crow Tears of the Indian police, had repeated by wire, with some words deleted by Western Union, that no Siksika, none, of the three Siksika Nations had ever lifted hair off anyone this far south in what Crow Tears called Sioux country. The Absaroke, or Crows, and Shoshone, or Horse Utes, had been the favorite enemies of his people in the Shining Times, but according to Crow

Tears they'd neither tangled seriously nor socialized all that much with the Sioux, no matter what the damned government records said.

Longarm digested his Siksika informant's version of Indian history with a grain of salt. He'd never caught Crow Tears in a flat-out fib. On the other hand, it seemed hardly likely that *all* the red and white army scouts who'd put Blackfoot in that unfortunately large encampment along the Little Bighorn could have been lying.

Custer and his command had stumbled into a gathering of Lakota, Cheyenne, Arapaho, and yes, Blackfoot, called together for a powwow by Tatanka Yatanka or Sitting Bull, the sort of Pope of the Lakota and their allies. Nobody had put down anything about, say, Kiowa or Comanche being present for the big hoedown of '76, even though they were at least as notorious as any fool Blackfoot. So whether Crow Tears liked to admit it or not, he hadn't accounted for *every* Blackfoot in this wicked world.

The Wind River Agency over to the west was even more adamant than Crow Tears, albeit more polite. They pointed out that despite a few bloody misunderstandings with their Saltu friends now and again, the Shoshone had scouted for the army against the infernal Sioux during Red Cloud's War, and hated the damned Blackfoot even more.

To Longarm's delicate suggestion that the mystery raiders might in fact be enemies of the Blackfoot, out to get them in Dutch with the Great White Father, the Shoshone police as well as their white agent replied, less delicately, that all their young men were present an accounted for. And so, if the raiders weren't really Blackfoot, they were likely damned old Sioux, up to old Sioux tricks in old Sioux country, as anyone but a deleted-by-Western-Union Saltu could see.

Longarm had covered that bet, of course. But the agent at Wounded Knee, on the Pine Ridge Reserve, not only vouched for all the important Lakota he could think of, but bitched about an impending Okipa or Sun Dance.

Longarm grimaced and muttered, "Right," as he put that wire aside. The horrendous rites around the Okipa pole had been forbidden by the B.I.A. more than once. The Lakota and some other Horse Indians went ahead and did penance to their

Wakans or Medicine Spirits anyway. For who was going to risk pissing off, say, Wakan Da, Wakan Yan, or Wakan Tanka just to avoid displeasing an all-too-human Great White Father?

Reading between the lines, as the agent he'd contacted had doubtless meant him to, Longarm agreed no Lakota out to count coup and make a name for himself would be apt to miss all the fun and bragging of a full-blown Okipa ceremony on the so-called Sioux Reserve. The wire hadn't said just how soon they figured to run up the pole and sharpen all the sticks for the dancers to stab their fool selves with. Longarm tried to recall all he'd ever seen, heard, or read in connection with the so-called Sun Dance. It was so messy in fact, and so distorted in legend, it was hard to say for certain whether Siksika went in for the same spiritual guidance. It seemed mighty unlikely any Lakota would dress up like a warrior of another nation if he meant to brag on recent coups while shuffling round the Okipa pole, singing up the rawhide lines he was dangling from as he let Wakan Da, the Sun Spirit, know how great he was. Few Indians felt it right to lie to other human beings, if it could be avoided. Lying to your Medicine Spirit while dancing and dangling on sharp stakes driven under the skin on your chest sounded like a way to meet up with old Okihadi, the Evil One, to Longarm.

On the other hand, he was neither an Indian nor given to twisting the truth beyond the bounds of logical thought. He had to allow that some wise-ass Indian could have talked a few pals into fibbing, just this once, so's they could put one over on the foolish Wasichu and . . .

"You must be that federal deputy," a gruff voice said, breaking his chain of thought, and when he glanced up, he saw he'd been joined by a tall drink of water wearing a brass badge, gun-barrel chaps, and a U.S. Army Issue Remington .45. As the local lawman stared down, neither friendly nor unfriendly, a boot of his own bracing his weight on the same wooden stairs, Longarm grinned up with his teeth gripping his half-smoked cheroot as he replied, "I'll admit to that if you'll admit to being Ross Larkin. Are you sore at me about something or just curious?"

Larkin smiled despite himself and sat down, saying, "I ain't sure. They tell me you run Woolly Bob Waterman outten town in my honor. I don't cotton to gents I don't know fighting for or agin me without my personal invite, Uncle Sam."

Longarm nodded soberly and replied, "I wouldn't either. I heard you'd had your own words with Woolly Bob. But to tell the pure truth, I can't say whether he's been running your brand or not of late. As that troublemaking barkeep should have explained, I got into it with the asshole without any help from anyone else. He simply started up with me, mayhaps for practice. I don't reckon he was expecting any poor wayfaring stranger to take him up on his kind offer with the enthusiasm I usually display at such times."

Larkin nodded again. "I've found it's usually best to get right down to brass tacks with a barroom bully too. It can save lots of fighting soft words don't seem to. Mahoney at the Elkhorn ain't the only one who told me how scary you can stare at five-to-one odds. I know your rep if you're the Deputy Long they call Longarm."

He shot a thoughtful glance at the ponies Longarm had tethered just down the way and added, "By this time Woolly Bob and his pals will have heard who backed 'em down last night. A man can walk away from a fight with an undistinguished drunk and just forget all about it. Crawfishing to the one and original Longarm is the sort of crawfishing legends are fashioned from, and while we both know Woolly Bob has a yellow streak, he's also got a .52 Plains rifle he can handle pretty good, and you did say you'd be riding on across the lonesome plains, didn't you?"

"I did," said Longarm. "Which way depends on what my home office wants me to do. I ain't finished my morning mail yet. I was sent up this way to figure whether your Indian trouble was a matter for the army or just a good spanking from the B.I.A. The farther I ride the more it looks like a chore for the boys in blue. You say you led that sweep across the open range yesterday?"

The local lawman and stock-raiser nodded and said, "I've already wired my own considered opinion to Fort Laramie. We lost their damn trail over by the buttes where the sod gives way to slick-rock. But then we backtracked the murderous sons of bitches to where they'd butchered and scalped a couple of white boys. As best we could read the other sign around their camp, some other whites must have got away. Four steel-shod ponies lit out from a nearby rise at a dead run, likely about the time the Blackfoot attacked their camp."

Longarm chuckled wryly and said, "I read sign wrong myself on occasion. In this case, though, I can tell you what you really read out by that scene of slaughter since I dropped by there earlier."

Ross Larkin listened with interest as Longarm brought him up to date on his recent adventures. He agreed the way Longarm put things together made more sense, but asked, "Why do you suspicion them two strangers was laying for you and that Baltimore gal when the Blackfoot hit 'em instead? You hadn't met up with Woolly Bob or anyone else up this way yet."

"Somebody more sneaky than your town bully could have known I was coming," Longarm pointed out.

"Well, *I* surely didn't," Larkin said. Longarm went on. "The B.I.A. did. So might anyone who'd reported Indian trouble to the B.I.A. and been assured they'd sent for someone smart as me. Back-checking on that could take more time than I can likely afford. So let's go with who'd have the best reason to stop me from finding out . . . what?"

Larkin looked uneasy and protested, "Don't look at me! I've told everyone I can think of that I need all the help I can get with the damned old Indians on the warpath. I can't think of anyone but Indians who'd be worried about you putting a stop to their wild ways."

Longarm shook his head. "Wild Indians seldom hire white gunslicks, and even when they do, they ain't inclined to kill 'em and lift their hair. So I'm inclined to go with a more civilized-looking mastermind with something mighty sneaky to hide."

He took a thoughtful drag on his cheroot, let it out slowly, and mused half to himself, "Has to be something federal or more tricky than your usual disturbances of the peace if they ain't been trying to bushwhack local lawmen like yourself— no offense."

As if to prove Longarm's point, Larkin said, "Ain't been much trouble, save for Indian trouble, before *you* showed up to scare the shit out of everyone last night."

Longarm frowned. "Do tell? Seems to me I heard tales of missing stock and your very own self accusing certain parties of running brands."

Larkin heaved an uneasy shrug. "I told you they make up legends about Woolly Bob every time he raises his voice in the Elkhorn. I don't know who told him I'd intimated an E-X-E could be run over a slash L mighty easy. When he demanded I either take him to law on it or apologize profuse, I told him not to talk like such an asshole and there the matter lies, for now. There ain't been no stock stealing since the Blackfoot showed up around here, as a matter of fact."

Longarm started to ask a dumb question. Then he nodded and said, "I spotted a wild buffalo alive and well the other day. So whatever them Indians are after, it ain't beef on the hoof. Likely just coups and horses to show off, if only I could figure where."

He started to tear open his telegram from Denver. Then he decided Larkin had to be more informed on local matters and asked, "What sent you and your posse out after 'em yesterday? Missing ponies?"

Larkin said, "Not exactly. Traveling man passing through said he'd been shot at coming up the Bozeman Trail from Douglas. They hit his pony instead of him. Not bad enough to stop the poor brute, though. He hurt it worse by lathering it close to ten miles at a dead run. One got the impression he'd been scared shitless. In any case, we felt obliged to saddle up and go after the red rascals."

"Did your spooked stranger really identify his assailants as Blackfoot, or even Indians?" asked Longarm, quietly.

Larkin thought before he decided. "Not in so many words, but who else . . . Oh, I see what you mean. But them two strangers who might have been after you were found miles away from where the traveling man said he'd been fired on."

Longarm smiled thinly and replied, "You just said he rode a good ten miles before anyone went looking for anybody, didn't you? Where's this traveling man right now, pard?"

Larkin said, "Traveling, of course. Said he took orders for the Excelsior Windmill Company. Doubt he sold many windmills here in Pumpkin Buttes. Know he swapped his wounded mount for a tolerable pony over to the Elkhorn, and last I heard, he'd lit out this morning for Crazy Woman. That's a town, not a deranged female, up where the Bozeman crosses Crazy Woman Creek."

Longarm nodded. "I know the place. It's over a day's ride from here, with or without trouble along the trail."

Larkin shrugged. "That's what we tried to tell him. But he allowed he was bent on selling more than one windmill to a big new outfit up yonder, and it's still a free country."

Larkin glanced up at the sun. "He's got better than a three-hour lead on you, but you might catch up with him at French Jenny's, the next trail town north. French Jenny ran a general store there. She was old and ugly besides."

Longarm chuckled. "I told you I've been through the Powder River country before, and she wasn't that bad before she died of the cholera that time. I ain't sure I ought to ride that far and fast just to hear what you've already told me about a person or persons unknown trying to bushwhack an apparently honest businessman on the trail."

But he got out his notebook and asked Larkin to give him a name and description just in case.

Larkin thought for a moment. "Said his name was Underwood, with some initials up front I don't recall. He looked about the way you'd expect a windmill drummer to look. A tad taller than average, somewhere in his middle thirties, and naturally dressed more business than cow."

"Did he sport a mustache, and how about his hat and saddle?" asked Longarm thoughtfully.

Larkin was turning out pretty smart for a part-time lawman. He shook his head and said, "Already considered that as soon as you told me someone seemed out to bushwhack *you* as well. Of course Underwood had a mustache. I just told you he was a full-growed gent trying to look businesslike. After that he didn't look all that much like you. His frock coat was dark gray, or a dusty black, and so was his hat. He rid in with a McClellan saddle, mounted on a bay that must have had some thoroughbred blood, like he said, since it kept on running long after a sensible cow pony would have quit with them two bullets in it."

Longarm sighed. "That ties it then. I'd best track down that poor bastard before someone else mistakes him for me, with better aim!"

Larkin objected, "I just said Underwood don't look at all like you, damn it."

To which Longarm could only reply, "Don't matter what he really looks like. He describes as a tall galoot wearing a frock coat and a mustache, and *I* left Douglas aboard a bay pony packing a McClellan saddle too. I'd never laid eyes on them two gunslicks I found dead on the prairie the other night. So they only had a description of me to go on and, unlucky for Underwood, they missed me."

Longarm rose to full height, adding, "I got to catch up with him before someone tries to kill me again."

Chapter 13

Longarm had picked up new trail supplies and lit out a good four or five miles before he got around to Billy Vail's latest instructions from Denver. He'd expected they might order him to turn the chore over to the army and head on home. That was only one of the reasons he'd waited till he was well on his way after the hapless windmill drummer called Underwood before he paused in a wooded draw to swap mounts, rest both a spell, and catch up on his reading.

They weren't too close to the original Bozeman Trail. Having been through the Powder River country before, in good times and bad, Longarm knew the lay of the land better than John Bozeman or even the army road builders who'd graded and improved the old military supply trace. So being anxious to overtake Underwood before someone less friendly might, Longarm had set a more beeline course for French Jenny's and to hell with a few steeper grades and brush-choked draws.

It wouldn't have been too smart to ride alone by daylight with at least one band of hostiles on the prowl either. Vail's wire said the railroad, the Postmaster General, and other interested parties had twisted arms at the B.I.A. and gotten Interior to agree War might as well round up the red sons of bitches Custer-style and let the commerce of the Plains get back to normal, dammit.

Vail said Longarm's old pal, Captain Matt Kincaid of the U.S. Dragoons, was on his way north from Fort Laramie with enough regulars to do the job, and he didn't, dammit, want Longarm offering to scout for the rascals.

Longarm knew he'd hardly have to. Matt Kincaid was good at hunting Indians, and while his methods weren't quite as draconian as those of the late George Armstrong Custer, Matt fought tough and mean enough. It had taken Longarm some time to gain the trust of the somewhat moody Crow Tears to begin with. It seemed a shame Longarm's kind and those of the good old Siksika had to go through all this bloody bullshit again, but sometimes that was the only way to resolve the Greek tragedy of the American Indian, there being bloody-minded assholes on both sides, and the clash of cultures being tough enough for *sensible* gents to thrash out.

Having rested and watered the bays he'd hired off Elsa Stern—Lord love her whether that had been her or not—Longarm rode on, following a contour line that kept his outline below the skyline while at the same time offering him a pretty good view of the ominously looming Pumpkin Buttes. The orange sandstone cliffs seemed to be keeping pace with him on the horizon as he rode at a mile-eating albeit uncomfortable trot. It made him miss his own McClellan, even as it explained why that windmill drummer ahead had picked the same brand of saddle. Underwood hadn't been out to get bushwhacked in another rider's place. As the assholes who'd tried to bushwhack the man should have known, a heap of gents more interested in distance than in roping cows chose old army saddles in the interests of both economy and comfort.

General George McClellan, a swell Quartermaster General and a blithering idiot in battle, had designed the saddle named after him with riding, not roping, in mind. The open slot one sat across let heat and moisture rise from the horse's unburdened spine, and wouldn't really endanger a rider's balls as long as his pants were as tight as a true horseman's pants were supposed to be.

Longarm's were, of course. He had to buy his ready-made tweed business suits in two sizes to leave his shoulders free for action and his crotch and lower limbs clad tight enough for serious riding or, if need be, running in his deliberately unfashionable low-heeled and spurless army stovepipes. He had to dress like an infernal townie because President Hayes and his first lady, Lemonade Lucy, seemed to think they were as fancy as Queen Victoria and her sissy hired help at Scotland Yard. Underwood was naturally wearing a similar business outfit because he was really out this way on business. Billy Vail had just told Longarm to drop his Indian investigation. He hadn't said anything about letting an innocent taxpayer get his fool self shot by mistake, and in any case, it hardly seemed any Indians had messed with the poor cuss to begin with.

"I'm missing something too," Longarm told his pony as he rode on to save a man he didn't know from who knows what. Bushwhackers had been out to stop Longarm before, usually for a far more obvious reason. Think back as he might, Longarm couldn't come up with anyone he'd jailed or shot it out with lately who'd be likely to have kith and kin out for revenge *this* serious.

The Plimmons brothers had been Colorado riders, it was true. But even if they'd hailed from a bigger and far broodier clan than indicated on their yellow sheets, how could anyone have sent anyone after anyone before the news of their half-ass attempt on that train could have made it's way first to someone with the weight to give such orders, and then back up the trail ahead to those willing to carry out such orders?

The Western Union clerk back in Pumpkin Buttes had assured him there'd been few wires sent in the past few days, because of that Indian scare, and that none of the few sent had mentioned Longarm or anyone else in an unfriendly way.

"The orders were given long before I got up this way," he informed his mount flatly, even as he noticed that left him no closer to any sensible solution.

Assuming someone had wired ahead as he was setting out on this mission, they'd had to have known, or thought they'd known, what his intended mission was.

"They must think I was sent out on another chore entire," he decided, resisting the impulse to reach for another smoke as he pressed on to the north-northwest. The day was shaping up to be another grass-burner, with the cloudless sky cobalt blue and crystal clear to the horizon. As if to prove his point he spotted dust, not much, but enough to read as someone riding hard along the Bozeman Trail, or some other trail as dusty, off to his left.

It was a free country, and as a rule he had to say in the use of a public right of way. But in times of Indian trouble any number of taxpaying citizens could be in the market for federal protection. So Longarm reined his mount to head the unseen but mighty dusty rider or riders off, glancing back from time to time to make sure only his trail supplies, and not near as much dust, were trailing after him.

By steering for a saddle in the long low rise between them and the lower ground the army road graders had chosen, Longarm was able to keep himself and his ponies off the skyline as he found that, as he'd expected, the wagon ruts of the Bozeman ran lonesome over that way save for a pair of riders headed lickety-split to the south on lathered ponies. Both the ponies and their hard riders appeared to be in the cattle business, albeit there wasn't a cow or any other critter in sight to inspire such apparent excitement. Neither rider seemed to notice Longarm as he sat his own pony, bemused, while they cut across his bow from right to left at half a mile or more. He was more interested in what in thunder might be chasing them. So he just watched, and watched till they were out of sight to the southeast and there was nothing to be seen along the Bozeman Trail but a slowly clearing haze.

Longarm shrugged, crawfished back through that same saddle in the ridge between the official trail and nowhere in particular, and rode on, humming "Farther Along" until, sure enough, he spied first the chimney smoke and then the tin or tar-paper rooftops of French Jenny's up ahead.

There wasn't that much chimney smoke, and no more than two dozen rooftops to the whole half-horse town. Like most such wide spots in the road, in this case the spot where the old Bozeman Trail swung close to the newer rail and telegraph lines, French Jenny's had sprouted from a water hole and patch of shade where a stove-up mountain man and his breed wife, French Jenny, had tried to homestead. When that didn't bring in any money, they'd commenced to peddle whiskey, matches, and other necessities to the passing public, red or white. Nobody recalled the handle of French Jenny's man, and as Longarm had

114

already noted, the old gal had been gone herself a good two years or more. But two years was a long time in the rapidly changing West of the postwar era. So now they had two saloons, four whorehouses, and other modern conveniences along the so-called Main Street running from the railroad platform to the original Bozeman Trail about three furlongs off to the west. As Longarm rode in he saw the long rise he'd been following was petering out in the acute angle formed by the trail and railroad as they swung ever closer together, so he drifted to his right to follow the service road running in line with the rails and telegraph line. He could see, long before he got there, that something exciting was taking place near the railroad water tower at the east end of town. Some of the milling figures spotted him at a distance too. So as he rode up to the last handy hitching rail and reined in to dismount, a peppery little cuss with a mail-order badge and ten-gauge market gun tore out of the crowd to throw down on Longarm and demand, "Reach for some sky and show me some identification, stranger!"

To which Longarm could only reply, "I'd be proud to if such a stunt was possible, pard. Since it ain't, I'd best assure you to begin with that I'm the law too. Federal. Would you really shoot me if I was to reach for that identification you just mentioned?"

The old-timer said, "Get down off that pony, slow, whilst I think about that. Lucky for you our most likely suspect was last seed forking a dapple gray mare."

Longarm stayed put aboard his bay as he frowned thoughtfully and replied, "Hold on. A cuss on a gray pony just tore past me in the company of another on a brown and white paint."

A younger but calmer-looking townsman who'd come close enough to hear that gasped, "They *was* a strange rider passing through on just such a paint, Deacon! Never connected him with that tinhorn riding the dapple gray, though!"

The oddly titled town law snapped, "Your lookout man ain't *supposed* to act like he's with you. I'll bet he was holding both their mounts, somewhere handy but outten sight, as his pal done the dirty deed."

He turned back to Longarm. "Which way did they go, how long ago, dammit?"

Longarm grimaced and said, "They're headed south, sudden, with too good a lead on us now. We'd be better off wiring Ross Larkin and his boys in Pumpkin Buttes. What did they do, rob your bank?"

Deacon shook his head and said, "We ain't got no bank. They just now backshot a U.S. deputy marshal. That famous one, calt Longarm!"

Chapter 14

Old Doc Miller, the local vet who doubled as deputy coroner and, in a pinch, set busted bones or delivered babies for human clients, had already determined the true identity of the late Fred Underwood by the time Longarm had identified himself to Deacon Dunvegan and persuaded the old-timer, now really confused, to show him the way to the smokehouse they were using as an ad hoc autopsy theater.

As Longarm shook hands with Doc Miller and his assistants in the gloomy smokehouse, he made a mental note not to order ham or smoked sausage for supper in French Jenny's. The freshly stripped and recently shot specimen laid out on pine planks across two sawhorses hadn't started to stink yet. But there was a strong scent of spoiled meat in the stuffy smokehouse, and when Longarm intimated it reminded him of a place called Shiloh, the jovial old vet said, "Yep. We had to open a mysterious Indian the boys found dead on the prairie a few days ago. He'd been out there a fair spell. So he was really ripe when we cut into him."

Longarm asked what had seemed most mysterious about the Indian. Doc Miller shrugged and said, "The probable cause. As far as I could make out, the son of a bitch just died out there. No wounds of any kind or symptoms of any usual ague. Indians die a heap from things we consider part of growing up. But there were no signs of chicken pox, mumps, or the whooping cough. He was too young for it to have been old age, and his heart seemed sound enough, save for being a mite decayed, like the rest of his innards."

Longarm asked if they could hazard a guess as to the nation of the poor rotting rascal. Doc Miller said, "Sioux, of course. This is Sioux country. Didn't you know that?"

Longarm assumed he knew as much as or more local history than any of the locals he'd talked to so far. He turned back to the unfortunate gent stretched naked on his belly so Doc Miller could get at the two blue holes between his shoulder blades. When Longarm asked what else they could tell him, aside from the fact that his wallet stuffed with business cards proclaimed him a salesman for that windmill company, the old vet cut cheerfully into the dead flesh with his scalpel, saying, "I was just about to go for the bullets, albeit more than one witness has already indicated he was shot twice, at close range, with a .45."

Deacon Dunvegan volunteered, "Army issue, single action. Ammo about as easy to trace as buffalo gnat eggs in the fly season. I wasn't there in the Yellow Rose myself, but the boys tell me this younger hand dressed cow and packing his Schofield low had been rawhiding the gent you see face down before you. I see now what nobody seemed to see then. The mean rider kept saying the famous Longarm didn't seem all that tough to him and Longarm—or in point of fact this other cuss entire—just seemed to make the kid madder every time he laughed and said he was a windmill drummer who'd never heard of any such person as the one the kid kept mentioning."

Another townie who'd worked his way in to watch volunteered, "I was there. Only heard a word of the argument, now and again. The kid wasn't all that young and innocent-looking, and I for one had heard a heap about a hardcase deputy who'd take just so much shit and not one fart further. I thought you, I mean him, was playing some sort of kid game with the kid. Not being a devotee of the sport myself, I've never savvied the delicate words the code duello seems to require of its participants. But I've spent me some Saturday nights in tougher saloons than the Yellow Rose in my time. So whenever I hear gents purring at one another in that oddly reasonable tone, I generally move outten their line of fire."

Longarm wrinkled his nose. "I've heard the long drawn-out bullshit you mean. I don't go in for it myself. It's the mark of a man arguing mostly with his own yellow streak, and it seems that in the end he shot this poor substitute for me in the back."

The one who seemed to know nodded and said, "Twice. I thought it was over when you, I mean that dead gent, raised his voice a mite and told the gun waddy he'd had just about enough of this bull. He said he was a dammit windmill drummer who'd come in to rest up over beer and sandwiches after a long dusty ride, and so the one pestering him went sort of pale and said he'd just been having fun and not to get sore. Then you, I mean the windmill drummer, told him to just go 'way and leave him the hell alone. So that's what everyone thought the killer meant to do when he nodded and headed for the door with a shit-eating grin. Then, just like that, he whirled around to whip his gun out and backshoot this cuss as he was biting into a ham on rye!"

Longarm stared soberly down at what had been meant to be his own dead corpse. It made a man feel odd, even when the gent filling in for the job hadn't looked all that much like him in life. The late Fred Underwood had stood about the same height as Longarm, but he'd been a softer, paler cuss, mayhaps a few years older, or more out of shape. His head lay in profile on the pine planks. A still-red pimple on one cheek made it tougher to tell he was dead, even though the nose had gone sort of waxy and the lips were already blue. Longarm said, "I'd be obliged if you could pump some formalin in him when you're done, Doc."

Miller held a small greasy object up to the lamplight, observing, "Common round, cut with a penknife to mushroom as it went through flesh. I *thought* it read like a hired assassin out to kill someone important for certain. I already meant to embalm this poor wayfaring stranger good. For he's a long way from home indeed, and his kith and kin will doubtless want the remains shipped east, with summer coming in."

Deacon Dunvegan said, "That reminds me. I was going to wire ahead to Pumpkin Buttes and I never did!"

But as he tore out in distress Longarm jogged after the older lawman to call out, soothingly, "Let's not get our bowels in an uproar, Deacon. They got a good ride ahead of them as well as a good lead. Both dots and dashes can get to the next town south way faster than even Pony Bob Haslan on his best day packing the mail."

Deacon slowed to a brisk walk, but fretted, "What if them two sons of bitches ain't headed for Pumpkin Buttes after murdering you—I mean that poor cuss they thought was you—for some reason?"

Keeping pace with the older and shorter man easily, Longarm replied, "If they're headed somewheres else, old Ross Larkin and his boys ain't likely to catch 'em. Let's hope them Indians do—the way they did a couple of other members of the same gang, I hope."

The town being so small, they got to the Western Union shed near the water tower before they could chew over the killing much more. Deacon Dunvegan didn't bother with any telegram forms. He just outright told the young clerk what he wanted sent sudden to the law down the line. The clerk asked him to repeat that description one more time. When he had, the Western Union kid said, "Now that's sure odd. But I'll get right on it."

Longarm, though younger, was apparently the more experienced lawman. He said, "Hold on, old son. What's so odd about that description? Seems to me two nondescript riders aboard a dapple gray and a paint can't be all that unusual in Wyoming Territory."

The clerk said, "Not as a rule, I reckon. But the very last wire out of here was sent by a cuss I took for a cowhand with a sick aunt. He had such ponies as you just described, tethered out front."

The town law demanded the exact time and whether the clerk was sure there'd only been one rider to go with those two ponies.

Longarm said, "Never mind. I saw two of 'em running those mounts past me over two hours ago. Let's talk about the wire you say the one of 'em sent from here, pard."

The telegraph clerk looked dubious and replied, "You got the time about right. It's against company policy to disclose

120

the messages sent by one customer to another."

Both lawman whipped out guns and Deacon snapped, "We're not customers, we're the *law,* Gawd damn your eyes!" so the clerk allowed that just this once it might be best to bend the rules a mite.

But the block-lettered message the clerk had long since wired down to the downtown Western Union office in Denver, across from the Union Depot, held far less information for them than Longarm had hoped.

The fact it was addressed to a Mister Johnson, care of Western Union, meant it had already been received by some son of a bitch who'd have hardly used his right name. The gist of the message was that someone's Aunt Ida was feeling a mite better and so there was no need for other family members to come running. It was signed simply "Joe," with no attempt to invent a last name. Longarm assumed, and the clerk agreed, that the mysterious Joe had taken his time composing the telegram and then sent it, at a nickel a word, by slapping down a silver dollar and leaving suddenly without having to wait for change.

When Deacon asked how he'd figured that, Longarm explained, "Twenty words, including Joe. He farted around till he heard shots in the distance and figured it was time to send it and meet up with someone else. Do you really need every move chalked on the blackboard for you?"

Deacon blinked and said, "Thunderation! That wire to Denver was a code message, telling someone down yonder they'd trailed you here and shot you dead! But how come?"

Longarm sighed. "I was sort of hoping you wouldn't ask that. But seeing I appear to be dead and don't have anyone gunning for me just now, what say we go find a cool place to sit and sip cider, or stronger, whilst we compare notes. I've been dying to find out why they call you Deacon when that badge reads Constable, for instance."

The older lawman said, "Hell, that's no mystery. I'm the deacon of the only church for miles as well as the only law in these parts. We can drink as cool cheaper, on my back veranda up the tracks. But don't you reckon you ought to wire your own office as long as we're here? If I was a Denver marshal with a deputy getting shot at, out in the field, I'd like to hear, from time to time, he's still alive."

Longarm nodded soberly. "I'm sure Marshal Vail would be reassured too. But for now I mean to keep my protracted existence a private matter. Nothing my own outfit can do for me from such a distance would be worth warm spit if the sons of bitches who just now killed me were to find out I was still alive. So for now, I'd best stay dead and see what happens next."

Chapter 15

All that happened, at first, was that Deacon walked Longarm back to where he'd tethered his own ponies, and then showed him the way to to his own place. There, sure enough, the veranda faced east, away from the afternoon sun, and Deacon's sort of young and pretty wife sent their sort of old and ugly housekeeper out to them from time to time with more eats to nibble with their tobacco and beer. Deacon surrendered his best rocker to Longarm, and rocked in a straighter-backed one on the far side of the tin table they were sharing, as Longarm brought him up to date on what the older lawman agreed to call a snarl of mighty mixed yarn.

When Longarm got to here and now, old Deacon sighed and said, "I'm sure glad nobody expects *me* to figure all that out. But I still got me some questions. I didn't want to mention it in front of young Casey at Western Union, but are you really worried about Western Union being in cahoots with . . . Just who might we be talking about?"

Longarm washed down the deep-fried chicken liver he'd been chewing with some tepid but tolerable suds before he replied. "If I could even make an educated guess, I'd know better whether they've been following me or heading me off.

123

We know they've sent at least one coded message about me by way of Western Union."

Deacon said, "Sure we do. But who'd be likely to read any wires you sent direct to your office in the Denver Federal Building, for Pete's sake?"

Longarm shrugged. "I just now said I didn't have the least notion. I've been sending and receiving wires, lots of wires, and we just proved how easy it is to intercept such messages if one really has a mind to. You don't have to throw down on a clerk with a gun if you want to be really sneaky. There's heaps of ways we don't have to waste time jawing about. Meanwhile, my home office has been wiring all over creation about me and those infernal Indians, so—"

Deacon interrupted him. "You just told me your department's dropping them Blackfoot and letting the army round 'em up."

Longarm nodded. "Billy tells me the army's coming up from Fort Laramie to put a stop to . . . whatever. That don't mean I can't still act as an interested party, as long as I'm up this way in any case. I can't help wondering how those two sets of wild men, red and white, fit together, if they do."

"They *can't* be in cahoots," Deacon objected. "White renegades have worked with bad Indians before, it's true. But I've never heard tell of even Blackfoot scalping comrades in arms!"

Longarm grimaced. "No Blackfoot are supposed to be out this summer scalping anybody anywhere. Did you ever have the feeling you were looking for something and couldn't see it, even though it was right in front of you, staring you in the face?"

The older lawman sighed. "Many a time. That wife I just introduced you to, inside, is my second one. My first wife was screwing our next-door neighbor right under my nose, and I'd have likely never found out if she hadn't got really sore at me one night and *bragged* about it."

Longarm smiled thinly. "Wives do that a lot. That's one reason I never mess with married women if it can be at all avoided. Getting back to white crooks trying to stop me whilst I've been trying to nip an Indian uprising in the bud, I keep staring and staring for some infernal *motive* their ringleader

124

ought to have in mind, and damn it, I'm just plain stuck."

Deacon smiled. "Don't feel ashamed, old son. All of us get stuck from time to time. I got dozens of stock-stealing cases and more than one murder unsolved. Nobody expects us to win 'em all."

"We're supposed to try," Longarm objected. "I was hoping I could get a fresh slant on recent events by telling you what I'd just been through. Sometimes, working too close to the trees, a lawman can miss the forest. Have you ever spent any time going over that case of the *Mary Celeste*, back in '72?"

The old-timer scowled and demanded, "Should I have? Are we jawing about that fool schooner they found abandoned in the middle of the ocean, for Gawd's sake?"

Longarm nodded. "Sure we are. Hasn't every lawman worth his salt considered such a famous mystery? Queen Victoria's famous detective, Proctor Flood, has written whole books on the investigation, and anyone can see that unless he missed something, the captain and crew of the *Mary Celeste* simply vanished into thin air in calm weather from a well-formed vessel—a brigantine, not a schooner, by the way. A lot of the sea yarns cribbed from the first reports describe the mystery vessel inaccurately too."

Deacon made a wry face and declared, "I don't care if it was a brigantine or a steamboat they found bobbing about with nobody aboard her. I told you I read about the case at the time. But like I said, I got enough on my own plate with missing stock and shootings like the one we just had over to the Yellow Rose. Seems to me that if fancy insurance dicks and queen's proctors couldn't solve the mystery of the *Mary Celeste*, it's just one of them mysteries as will never be solved, right?"

"Wrong," said Longarm. "The answer's so blamed obvious I'd have made my arrests long ago if I'd been in charge of the investigation. Only I was riding for the Justice Department, and no doubt the famous English detective who blamed it all on spooks knew even less than me about marine insurance. It was a simple case of deliberate fraud by persons known—to wit, Captain Benjamin Briggs of the *Mary Celeste* and Captain David Morehouse of the British-owned *Dei Gratia*, who found the *Mary Celeste* abandoned and adrift off the Azores, he said.

All the bullshit about mysterious marks on the railing of the *Mary Celeste* and whether there were signs of struggle or not become moot as soon as you figure who done it and why."

Deacon Dunvegan stared thunder struck across the table. "How did you find all that out, Longarm? Are you saying you took part in that investigation back in '72?"

Longarm shook his head. "Nope. I was just breaking in with Billy Vail at the time. I wouldn't know the *Mary Celeste* if she come sailing across yonder prairie at us, and I've no idea what either of those crooked captains looked like, save that Briggs of the *Mary Celeste* was mighty young to put in command of even a brigantine when he vanished forever—so convenient for his business partner, David Morehouse. You see, what Proctor Flood never saw fit to look into, all the time he was searching for pirates, ghosts, sea monsters, and such, was who might or might not have had *a motive* to stage a sort of half-ass marine disaster, as soon as you study the fine print."

"Well, read me the fine print then!" Deacon demanded.

So Longarm leaned back expansively to explain. "Briggs sailed the *Mary Celeste* from the port of New York in the fall of '72, bound for Italy with a cargo of industrial alcohol. She'd been tied up to the same dock as the British brigantine *Dei Gratia,* commanded by the aforementioned David Morehouse, a close friend of young Briggs and his wife."

Deacon blinked. "The *Mary Celeste* was found abandoned by a *knowed associate* of the *skipper,* and them limey detectives never wondered about that?"

Longarm nodded. "It gets better. Morehouse was more than a pal of Briggs. He was part owner of the *Mary Celeste,* and she'd been insured, most naturally, by her owners. How do you like it so far?"

The older lawman laughed like hell and said, "Jesus H. Christ, I'd have arrested Morehouse too! But hold on, if the ship he'd insured was found still afloat, with her cargo intact . . ."

"Salvage fees," Longarm explained, "That's how I figure young Briggs, his wife, and at least his mate had to be in on it. If they'd all gone down with the *Mary Celeste,* Morehouse would have collected even more from the insurance underwriters. So it's more likely nobody taking part in the fraud had the stomach for murder. Morehouse and his *Dei Gratia* left New York just after the *Mary Celeste,* so's to catch up with her west of the Azores before anyone else might. I can't say whether Briggs and his bunch simply put a boat over the side and headed for the nearby Azores, or whether, even easier, they just boarded the *Dei Gratia* to swap places with her salvage crew and—"

"Some of 'em could have *been* that salvage crew!" Deacon shouted, now more interested. "It works most simple if all aboard both vessels were in on it. Neither would have needed all that big a crew to begin with, names are easy to add and subtract from a ship's log, and hell, nobody began any investigation till *after* both the *Dei Gratia* and *Mary Celeste* had put in to shore."

"Nowheres near one another." Longarm laughed. "Captain Morehouse's salvage crew, whoever they might have been, sailed the *Mary Celeste* on to Gibraltar and turned her over to the British Navy while the *Dei Gratia* went on to her own ports of call, dropping off her own cargo and any passengers the captain might or might not have had listed. Like I said, Morehouse received a handsome salvage free from the doubtless grateful insurance underwriters, and meanwhile, neither he nor any of the other owners of the *Mary Celeste* were out a nickel."

Deacon smiled dubiously and allowed Longarm's notion had sea monsters or even unusually gentle pirates beat, but pointed out, "That was still a swamping secret for at least two dozen men and one woman to keep."

Longarm shrugged. "At least that many know the present whereabouts of Frank and Jesse James and, so far, nobody's come forward to collect the considerable reward on those cute rascals."

He sipped some more suds and added, "There was no reward posted on the invisible octopus or whatever, and nobody ever checked up on the crew members Captain Morehouse put ashore here, there, and Lord knows. Anyone coming forward, at this late date, would have to implicate his or herself in a hoax calling for at least a few years at hard in Dartmore Prison. Queen's proctors can get testy as all get-out when you make 'em look unprofessional."

Deacon shrugged. "I'm sure glad we've cleared that case up. What's the mystery of the *Mary Celeste* got to do with the cowboys and Indians you've been having so much trouble with more recent?"

Longarm sighed. "I was sort of hoping I wouldn't have to answer that half as good just yet. My point is that Proctor Flood missed the obvious and simple by climbing all over the *Mary Celeste* with his magnifying glass, searching for sea-monster sign. I got this gnawing hunch that I'm starting right through the obvious answers by trying to make sense of the unsensible."

When Deacon asked, in that case, what the obvious answer might be, Longarm snorted in disgust. "Ain't you been paying any attention at all? If I had the least notion what this was all about, I'd be making me some arrests instead of riding up and down the Bozeman Trail like a chicken with my head cut off! Quill Indians tend to have different motives than your average white crook. So I'll go along with the ones raising Ned in these parts being out for ponies and other such brags. But that's where they part company with any white mastermind trying to protect them from me. Everyone tells me that since these Indian troubles commenced a few weeks ago, *other* troubles in the Powder River country have just about died away total!"

Deacon nodded. "You can't rob a train or even a stage with neither running because of the Blackfoot menace. A few ponies have been run off, as you just suggested, but the outfits had just finished the spring roundup when the scare commenced and, so far, the herds all seem to be about where they was when their owners cut and branded so recent."

Longarm didn't speak. So they were just sort of sitting there when a kid in bib overalls came along the cinder path to bawl, "The doc wants to know what you want him to do with that dead drummer now that he's signed the danged papers and it ain't getting any cooler in that smokehouse."

The old lawman rose, wearily, to bawl back, "I'm coming, dammit. Seems I have to do everything around here, what with my church and law-enforcing duties. How's about yourself, Deputy Long?"

Longarm said, "I'll be along directly. First I got to stable these two ponies and mayhaps find a place where I can lay my own head just a few winks. I don't want to ride alone by

128

daylight, now that I see I don't have to, and a man has to sleep *some* damned time."

Deacon nodded curtly. "You don't have to search all that far. Carry them ponies around to the north and run 'em in with mine. You'll find cracked corn and fresh hay in our stable loft. If the watering trough in the stalls is dry, my own stock and me would be obliged if you'd give the pump handle a few good cranks. Meanwhile, I'll tell the gals inside to put you in our guest room and leave you alone till suppertime, hear?"

They shook on that and parted friendly. As Deacon went into the house, Longarm untethered the two bays and led them afoot around the north end of the house until, sure enough, he spied a lower-slung stable with sod walls and a tin roof. There was a corral, and then a grassy paddock as well. But the sun was way high now, and so Longarm wasn't surprised to find Deacon's three ponies and an old tabby cat inside the stable soaking up some shade. He put his own stock in two adjoining stalls, hung the pack and riding saddles over the rail of another, and rubbed both bays down with some handy rucksacking. There was already plenty of water in the long trough running the length of the stalls. Longarm pumped cooler ground water into it anyway, before he rustled up a hatful of grain and a double armful of fresh-cured love-grass hay.

Then, the needs of his ponies attended to, Longarm strode back to the house to see about Deacon's even kinder offer.

The man of the house had apparently told the gals he'd birch them good if they didn't take good care of their guest from Denver. The homely and surely hatchet-faced housekeeper smiled so hard she almost managed to look pretty, and old Deacon's already pretty young wife looked downright wicked as, discovering they couldn't tempt him with more refreshments, she allowed he had to be exhausted, poor thing, and led him to a clean cozy upstairs room he suspected she kept mostly to brag on. The four-poster bed was covered in pink chenille, and worse yet, one of those leggy French rag dolls reclined against the fluffed pillows, dressed in one of those sassy can-can outfits, fluffy drawers and all. Flora, as she said she liked to be called because Mrs. Dunvegan sounded so stuffy, closed the shutters and pulled the blind of the one dormer window, plunging the hitherto bright sunny room into a gloom the exact shade of beef gravy. But he could still see the way her big eyes glistened as she turned to him after picking up the rag doll and whipping down a corner of the covers for him. She said, in a somewhat mocking if not downright dirty tone, "I don't think I ought to leave Fifi alone up here with anyone young and handsome as you, ah, Custis. Fifi's been feeling sort of desperate of late, if you follow my meaning."

He was afraid he did. But he tried to sound more rustic as he soberly replied, "I wouldn't know much about the feelings of rag dollies, ma'am. My folks never encouraged me to play with dollies growing up. I reckon they worried I'd wind up with foolish notions about such matters as you ascribe to that there play-pretty."

She sighed and ventured, "What would you say, or do, if faced with a real live girl who's been feeling sort of neglected of late?"

He kept his voice as innocent, but let his gun-muzzle gray eyes meet her unwavering stare icily as he replied, "That's not easy to answer, Miss Flora. Are you saying your housekeeper downstairs has expressed a mad desire for my fair white body?"

Flora Dunvegan laughed incredulously and replied, "For your what, you big oaf? Poor old Bess is old enough to be your mother, and a confirmed virgin besides!"

Longarm smiled back, thinly, and said, "*Bueno*. In that case I feel ever so much safer up here, knowing neither your housekeeper nor your rag dollie really mean to get fresh with me."

"Haven't you forgotten someone?" Flora purred.

He shook his head firmly and said, "Not hardly, Miss Flora. A man would have to be *loco en la cabeza* to entertain wicked thoughts about rag dollies, old maids, or . . . married women."

She pouted her lower lip at him and hugged her dumb doll closer to her considerable breastworks, murmuring, "Some men I know aren't such big sissies about such minor barriers to, well, a nice little quickie with a girl who enjoys such harmless games."

Longarm didn't bother to hide his feelings all that much as he coldly informed her, "Some men you know likely steal from the poor box in your husband's church, when he ain't looking, too. I know how harmless such games can get, Miss Flora. As the arresting officer, more than once, I've often felt the so-called victims had it coming."

She stamped her foot. "Easy for you to say. You don't know what it's like to be stuck with an old goat who's not that grand a lover on the rare occasions he can get it up!"

"Since we're talking so frank," he replied in a calmer tone, "I'd like to assure you I'd sure hate to be married up with some old gal I didn't enjoy going to bed with either. That's doubtless why I've never married up with anyone I figured I could live without. If and when I do get hitched, I aim to abide by the terms of the contract whether I feel like it or not. I figure a deal is a deal. I got more respect for an honest whore than I do a so-called respectable gal who'd wed an old man just to have him feed and clothe her good so's she could fool around as usual with bums who ain't even paying her."

She slapped his face and flounced out of the room. He'd sort of expected her to, since those first few sly remarks. He stared wistfully down at the tempting four-poster. The clean sheets stank of lavender, and there was a good solid door-bolt to temp him further. But, as he'd just told her, he'd been the arresting officer more than once, and that poet who'd remarked on Hell having no fury to compare with a pissed-off female had likely turned a few of 'em down in his day.

So he was fixing to go, without the least notion where, when that door Flora had just slammed behind her popped back open and old Bess, the spinsterish housekeeper, slipped in to announce, "You could be in a whole lot of trouble if that vixen's headed where I fear she might be, cowboy!"

Longarm smiled sheepishly down at her to reply, "I ain't no cowboy. But I doubt even my federal badge would help if she's run off to tell her old man I just made a play for her French dolly!"

Bess dimpled her somewhat craggy face and assured him, "Deacon's less likely to gun you in defense of Fifi's honor, or mine, than he is for trifling with his Flora! He caught his *first* wife in bed with another man and it almost killed him!"

"What did it do to the other man?" asked Longarm, dryly.

131

Bess said, "We don't like to talk about that. Suffice it to say, Deacon has a temper to match his shotgun if he's really pushed, and even if you won . . ."

"I know he's their deacon as well as their elected law," Longarm said. "I was just about to light out for parts unknown, damn her wagging tongue and other parts! Just give me a few more seconds in the shade to figure which way I want to ride."

She said, "You don't *want* to ride out of town in any direction with those Blackfoot on the prowl. Are you open to a more sensible suggestion, if I promise not to, ah, get silly about it?"

He told her to get silly as she wanted, as long as it got him out of this dumb fix. So the craggy-faced and sort of skinny old gal shut the door behind her, leaving it unbarred, and said, "First we get in bed together. He could barge in here any moment, and we have to offer him convincing proof at first glance, see?"

Longarm did. He forced himself to stop laughing quite so hard when he saw he seemed to be hurting her feelings. He said, "I ain't laughing at the thought of you and me in bed together, Miss Bess. I'm laughing at the scene that's sure to follow when and if old Deacon finds us in any such compromising position."

She nodded. "He'll surely be more inclined to smile than shoot. Let me do the talking after that. I've already got it straight in my head how hysterical Flora got when you chose me instead of her just now, and how mean it was of her to try and get us all in trouble with all those big fibs, right?"

Longarm started to say something dumb. Then he reached a decision. "Right. An old man catching his young wife in a vicious act of sheer stupidity shouldn't feel half as stupid as he might the other way. But what about you, your job, your reputation, Miss Bess?"

The gal they'd all had down as a hopeless old maid proceeded to unpin her mousy brown hair as she demurely replied, "Get undressed, at least partway, for Pete's sake, and we'll talk about it in bed."

So he shucked most of his duds to get into the four-poster in his summer-weight underdrawers with his weaponry handy on the lamp table, while old Bess peeled off her print dress

132

to climb in beside him dressed like Lady Godiva in nothing but her surprisingly long brown hair. It didn't look quite so drab, unbound with turgid nipples peeking through it. As she raised the covers on her side to slide her bare body in with his, he noticed that while her face didn't look all that much younger in the kinder light, her long slim body looked like that of a tomboy with a little filling-out left to do. She smelled mighty tempting too, whether that was her natural smell or just some stink-pretty she'd put on downstairs. He was hoping she'd prepared in advance for this unexpected visit. It was the sort of question a man hesitated to ask, even when a gal was obviously younger and hence more likely to go to bed reckless.

He reached out to reel her in, almost without thinking, for who spent much time *thinking* when a lady first climbed into bed with him? But even though she snuggled her bare tits against his bare chest mighty temptingly, she protested, "Wait, we have to get out stories down pat."

He chuckled and asked, "What stories? What would you think if you come through yonder door to catch two naked adults of opposing genders in this bed like this?"

"I have," she said. "Flora's taken some awful chances since I've been working for them. I don't care if this gets me fired. I'd as soon work for more respectable, or at least less stupid, folk. As for my reputation, I can't see that vixen bragging about me taking a man away from her like this, can you?"

He thought. "Nope. No way old Deacon can gossip all that much without looking sort of odd too, come to study on it. But now that we've saved everyone's lives at this cost to your shy nature, Miss Bess, where in thunder could the old coot and his shotgun be this late in the game?"

She snuggled closer, assuring him, "It's only been a few minutes. He may want to liquor himself up to a full head of steam first, and then again, Flora might have only run off to seek solace with the village blacksmith. Again."

He asked if the cheating wife of a man he liked did that a lot, and Bess replied, "Too often for her own safety, if you ask me. Sooner or later she has to get caught, and some of the wives of those other men are more likely to kill her, dirty, than poor old Deacon!"

133

Longarm repressed a shudder. "Well, I already told her what I thought of her harmless fun, as she calls it. I sure wish I knew whether we figured to have armed and dangerous company any damned minute. My first intentions towards this bed involved some shut-eye, and that was before I felt how soft it was."

She sighed and said, "Close your eyes and go to sleep then. I'll keep watch and wake you the moment I hear anyone coming. I'm not at all sleepy. As a matter of fact I feel unusually wide awake. It's not every day an old bat like me finds herself naked in bed with a handsome stranger."

He said, "Aw, you ain't such a bat and you can't be much older than me, Miss Bess. As a matter of fact, if that door was barred and I knew you weren't just trying to save my fool hide, I'd likely get sort of, well, wide awake myself."

So old Bess slid out her side of the bed, padded over to the door stark naked in the dusky but not that dusky light, and slid the brass bolt firmly shut before she turned to face him in the altogether and murmur, "Wake up then." She came calmly back to bed and ripped the covers off him completely.

He had to slide his underdrawers off first, as she slipped a firm pillow under her slender hips and lay back as if they were old friends who'd had afternoon orgies before. But as he cocked a leg over to get his bare hips between her widely welcoming thighs, he felt sure that if he'd ever passed this way before he'd have surely remembered. For while kissing her plain face felt sort of dumb at first, she was put together like a young woman, a very young woman, where it really counted. He was only saved from feeling like a cradle-robber by the way she moved those obviously experienced hips and gripped his old organ-grinder with her soft but strong internal flesh. As he shot his wad suddenly, but kept on churning in her creamery, the sweet-screwing Bess sobbed, "Oh, thank you, thank you for what you just did, and thank you even more for not stopping! But do you really enjoy doing it this way with such an old silly?"

He hooked an elbow under each of her long slender limbs to pose her sort of like that French rag dolly doing a can-can split as he replied that it was always sort of silly, with anybody, and didn't it still feel swell? So she shut her mouth as well as her eyes and enjoyed a sort of tooth-grinding fit as he just ground her good until he'd made her come and apparently crippled her for life, to hear her moaning and groaning about how deeply she'd felt all that affection.

He figured she'd forgiven him when she shyly announced she'd like to get on top and see if they could get it even deeper that way. So he let her and they could, or rather, she could, once she'd moved into a sort of flat-footed squat atop him, bouncing her tiny buttocks between his hips in a manner that threatened to crash them both through the bed springs.

When he warned her of that possible disaster, she just laughed and asked if he'd ever screwed this hard before. But he knew she didn't really want to hear about that huskier Mex gal down Denver way that time, and somehow the four-poster survived her enthusiasm, and hell, he even caught a few winks in it afterwards. He didn't remember dozing off. He never did. But the next he knew she was waking him to warn him it was almost suppertime and that, so far, nobody had come up the stairs outside with or without a gun.

He said that likely meant old Flora had gone off to get laid instead of in search of revenge. Bess agreed, and shyly asked if he was sore about her getting in bed with him without a better reason.

He kissed her sincerely and growled, "There ain't no better reason to get in bed. Lay back and let me show you some hard feelings to prove I ain't sore, little darling."

Chapter 16

All things considered, both Flora Dunvegan and her spinster housekeeper sure looked as if they'd spent an uneventful day as they ate supper an hour later with Longarm and old Deacon. When Longarm said he sure admired the mashed potatoes, Flora said Bess had mashed them, and Bess smiled right at him when he had to say she surely mashed fine. Old Deacon simply asked someone to pass the salt, and when his young wife said too much salt was bad for him, the old man told her not to use any then. So what with one such comment here and so many odd smiles there, supper took something like a million years.

After a smoke on the veranda while the two gals cleared the table inside, old Deacon suggested they drift over to the Yellow Rose for some real dessert and Longarm, seeing the sun hadn't nearly finished setting, agreed. He hankered for starlight more than he needed a beer on top of all that home cooking, but next to a barbershop a small-town saloon offered nigh as much gossip as a neighbor gal hanging her laundry out to dry, and right now, Longarm felt mighty open to suggestions.

He had not, in truth, made up his mind which way he meant to ride that night. But once Deacon had introduced him to some of the other important townies, and once they'd all seemed to think he'd be pressing on north toward, say, Buffalo Town, where those pesky Blackfoot had first been spotted, Longarm allowed that was the way he was heading, even as he was considering another destination entirely.

To begin with, that Indian band hadn't been spotted any particular place since Longarm's personal brush with them, even though he seemed to be the only white man in Wyoming Territory who couldn't say which way they went with that one serious casualty. Longarm did know that unlike the U.S. Army, Horse Indians took casualties seriously. Raised to view warfare as the natural condition of mankind, they were as brave as or braver than your average seasoned trooper. But while white folks believed in luck, good or bad, Indians who followed the old-time religion preached by gents shaking rattles viewed most everything that happened as medicine, or the influence of spirits.

There was nothing more ferocious than a Horse Indian riding with the certain knowledge that since his feathers and paint were just so and his war dance had been performed just right, he had to be in good with Wakan Tanka or, in the case of Blackfoot, Manitou.

Like a Saracen riding against Crusaders in the firm conviction he was out to strike a blow for an approving Allah, a Horse Indian coming at you in full feathers and paint was capable of suicidal heroics, unless and until somebody shook his faith in his medicine. Once that happened all bets were off and Mister Lo could pull most any surprising stunts.

At Little Bighorn the Indians had kept coming despite heavy casualties among the so-called Suicide Society charging up Last Stand Ridge on foot. A Lakota Longarm had asked about that had explained that the bad medicine of a old boys from another band hadn't discouraged the mounted followers of Crazy Horse as they'd charged along that same rise to steamroller Custer and his command from their vulnerable flank. The few casualties Crazy Horse's old boys took in the process were plainly outweighed by the encouraging sights and sounds of shot-up Wasichu. They could see their medicine was better, and their old-time religion provided for some battle losses as long as the enemy was getting clobbered in the process.

Things were not supposed to go the other way. No Indian nation Longarm had ever heard of would hold up a fight like the

137

one at The Alamo as an example of anything but heap bad medicine. At the Battle of Beecher Island back in '68 the Cheyenne had fought like rabid wolverines, and the whites pinned down on a sand bar in the middle of a knee-deep prairie stream were done for till a lucky shot spilled the mighty Roman Nose and seemed to knock all the wind out of the Indians' sails.

Whites who should have known better, even some who'd been there, still said the old boys at Beecher Island had been saved because the Indians had lost their leader. That wasn't what the Cheyenne had lost. They'd lost their medicine. Just before riding out to attack that army column Roman Nose had gone through special purification rites. He'd just found out he'd eaten some buffalo stew stirred with an *iron fork* by a stupid or treacherous captive woman, and everybody knew how *that* could fuck up a man's medicine!

So when Roman Nose got his fool self killed at Beecher Island, after all the trouble everyone had gone to with steamed herbs, tobacco smoke, and genuine box-turtle rattles, his followers could plainly see he was sure in bad with Manitou, and as every one knows, such curses can be catching.

So Longarm just couldn't say whether those old boys he'd brushed with were likely to seek revenge or head for home discouraged. He had no notion where they'd be this evening in any case.

Men at the bar who'd yet to swap shots with any Indian were naturally more certain about such matters. A middle-aged storekeeper with a gold tooth opined, "They'll be streaking north, back to Blackfoot Country, if they know what's good for 'em. The army can do forty miles a day if it wants, and I hear tell a whole brigade of dragoons has already left Fort Laramie!"

Longarm was nursing his beer, not wanting to take piss breaks along the trail when his ponies didn't need the rest. So he lit a fresh smoke and got rid of the match in a handy spittoon against the base of the bar before he said, "More like a dragoon company with a captain in command. But you're likely correct in assuming no more than two dozen Indians will want to avoid 'em. As to whether they'll vacate this range entirely, that's a whole other wager. Mister Lo has this annoying habit of choosing another partner when he don't want to dance with

138

you. I'd keep my eyes open and my powder dry if I was you boys and the weather was just getting right for hit-and-run raiding."

Somebody asked what Longarm meant. Old Deacon proved he knew his own ass from his elbow by snorting in disgust and announcing, "Harder to track hoofprints as the ground bakes harder and the grass turns to tougher straw. Them dragoons will have their chores cut out for 'em indeed if they don't cut Mister Lo's trail this side of the Glorious Fourth!"

Gold Tooth protested Deacon's pessimism, and allowed he'd refuse to pay taxes if the damned fool army let the Indians run loose as late as the month of July. Another optimist declared, "They're likely on the run already. The railroad's already fixing to resume operations in these parts."

Longarm hadn't heard that either, so he studied the informative cuss as he rambled on. Longarm recalled him as one of the townies who'd been running telegrams back and forth for Deacon earlier as the man explained, "Got it from the freight dispatcher down to Pumpkin Buttes. He got it off these railroad inspectors who come up from Douglas, by buckboard, of course. They say they got to look the roadbed and the Indian situation over before they send any locomotive poking its timid cowcatcher our way."

That made too much sense to be worth following up on, but it did remind Longarm of earlier wires. He turned to Deacon and said, "I assume you'd have told me if those two galoots we suspect as the killers of poor old Underwood showed up anywheres down the line, right?"

Deacon nodded. "I would have. I reckon that, not unlike them Indians, they've chose to ride around such places as they might be expected to ride through. We sure got a tedious amount of open range to ride around on in these parts."

Longarm said he'd noticed that, and polished off the last of his one long schooner of draft. When he said he had to be on his way, Deacon offered to walk him back to the stable, adding, "I ain't sure I ought to let you ride out alone, old son. Them soldiers coming from the south ought to encourage them Indians to head north, along the very trail you've been talking about."

Longarm shook his head. "I can find my way to my ponies without anyone holding my hand, Deacon. I doubt them Indians will be dumb enough to ride the Bozeman itself. I know *I* won't. I'd be obliged if nobody here wired ahead about me riding anywheres, hear?"

Deacon nodded. "I follow your drift. I'd be obliged if you'd wire me, later, and let me know who seemed most surprised to discover you hadn't been backshot after all. But do you really expect to catch up with your mysterious enemy up to the north? Them gunslicks you spotted were headed south, and have you forgot one of 'em wired Denver just as Underwood lay dying?"

Longarm said, "I'll look into that once I'm back in Denver. Meanwhile, I was sent up this way to scout them Indians, and like everyone says, north is the logical way one would expect Blackfoot to be headed, if they're headed home at all."

They shook on it and parted friendly in the doorway, Longarm to head for his ponies and Deacon to head back to the bar and finish his after-supper relaxation.

Longarm avoided the Dunvegan house as he circled around to the stable. Parting might be such sweet sorrow to some, but he'd always found it a pain in the ass. So he saddled up in the dark and led the ponies out afoot, to mount up and ride north along the railroad service road, at first, in case anyone cared.

Then, as the last pinpoint of lamplight from some upstairs window back there winked out behind a gentle rise, Longarm swung east across the tracks and kept going till the only features he had to steer by were the brightly winking stars above. Then he headed south with the Big Dipper peering south over his shoulder. He knew it was a sin to tell a lie, unless one had to. Deacon and the few others who knew he was still alive seemed good old boys he could trust with such secrets. But he wouldn't *have* to trust them if they all had him figured for a northbound lonesome rider.

Those Indians could be headed back to Blackfoot Country, or hell, Constantinople, as far as Billy Vail cared now. Longarm was still interested, being curious by nature to begin with and not too pleased with Washington's current Indian policy either. But he'd *tried* to do things delicately for the B.I.A., and there were times it just couldn't be done that way. This particular band had spilt blood, and vice versa. Neither side was going to be satisfied as things now stood. President Hayes and Little Big

Eyes were a far cry from the bloody-minded Indian Ring of the Grant Administration. But they'd still insist on a few good examples shot or hanged by the neck until dead, dead, dead.

Longarm knew his old pal, Captain Kincaid, would treat the Indians as fair as possible. How fair might be possible was the rub. Longarm had plenty of Siksika pals too, and he knew just how reasonably good old boys like Crow Tears were apt to behave when and if Siksika kissing cousins wound up getting killed, or worse yet, strung up for murder—as the government insisted on calling good clean fun on the part of restless red youths.

As he rode along, Longarm hoped Kincaid would simply smoke up some and run the rest home to lick their wounds. That was as close to a peaceable end to an Indian rising as one could hope for. A warrior was supposed to avenge his own defeats and, once he was defeated good enough, he sometimes chose to forgive and forget, or at least forgive. Neither elephants nor Indians ever *forgot*, and while the white man considered hanging a merciful form of execution, Indians thought it was just awful. Even nations who'd never liked the so-called Sioux thought that the mass hanging of Little Crow's followers in the wake of the big uprising of '62 ranked on a par with the burning of Joan of Arc, if not Herod's Massacre of the Innocents. You likely had to be an Indian to savvy why hanging seemed too horrid next to, say, being poked to death with sharp sticks or eaten alive by ants. Longarm only knew they thought it was, but hell, old Matt Kincaid knew that too. He'd likely shoot as many as he had to and let the others get away to spread the word about bad medicine this summer. You ate an apple a bite at a time, and dealt with Indian risings as they rose. Right now, even if Billy Vail hadn't ordered him to let the fool army have the fool Indians, Longarm was more interested in those *white* sons of bitches he'd been having trouble with. More importantly, he was interested in *why*.

There was nobody else a federal lawman could turn white killers of the civilian persuasion over to. He had to find out what they didn't want him looking into before he could even consider forgiving them for killing him at least once and trying to way more often. He thought back, and realized his trouble with them had started after he'd left Denver, not before, when any number of assholes could have pegged a backshot at him on his way to or from the office.

That had happened to him a lot in the past. So far, it had either been an attempt at revenge or, as often, an attempt to keep him from catching some son of a bitch.

Revenge would have seemed as simple and far safer on the crowded streets of Denver. But who in blue blazes could they be trying to protect by gunning him out on the prairie while he was, dammit, scouting Indians and . . . who else?

He reined in, dismounted, and got rid of some of that damned beer as he decided there hadn't *been* anyone else. Aside from a few slightly naughty females, who hadn't busted any federal laws as far as he could see, Lord bless 'em all, nobody up this way had even busted a local ordinance, save for those obvious henchmen of his unknown enemy, who'd been acting even meaner than those mysterious Indians.

"I wish I could make things fit together that way." he said aloud, remounting to ride on as he explained to his pony, "This Indian scare has made it damn near impossible to rob a train or run off stock. A mastermind well heeled enough to fund such long-range skullduggery by wire could have something like a land grab in mind, and that works better with staged Indian raids, till you consider how few folks there are up here to scare away. More than nine tenths of Wyoming Territory is still unclaimed federal land, and them dragoons on their way this very minute prove how difficult it is to scare the federal government off its land with a handful of so-called Indians!"

He pondered that point for perhaps a furlong, deciding in the end that whatever nation they were from, those quill Indians he'd brushed with to the south, the way he was headed, had been the genuine article. It was harder for a white man to pass for an Indian within rifle range than some thought. The two races were built different, rode different, and didn't yell at all the same. The old Rebel yell could sound sort of bloodcurdling, yelled right by a good old boy full of corn squeezings. But it didn't sound the same as say that turkey-gobble war cry of the Nadene, the kicked-pup yipping of a Pawnee, or the laughing-jackass taunts of the Lakota.

Longarm took a tighter bearing on a southern constellation as he thought back and muttered aloud, "Them redskins me and

Crow Mary brushed with brayed jackass-style as they charged. Cheyenne and Arapaho seem to have picked up the same bad habits from their Lakota allies. But what are Siksika supposed to yell like, dammit?"

It was his own fault, he knew, for having been so friendly with the Blackfoot police he'd met up with, long after the unhappy events of '76. It was still safe to say those old boys he'd swapped lead with this season had looked like Horse Indians, ridden like Horse Indians, and yelled like Horse Indians from one damned nation or another.

That one old boy daring death with his death song so as to recover the body of a fallen comrade read more quill Indian than some white boy playing at it too. So . . .

"We are thinking in circles and such shit must cease!" Longarm announced, suddenly and loudly enough to spook his mount. As he reined in to pat its neck and steady it, he saw they'd drifted a mite to the east again. He was aiming to ride into Pumpkin Buttes out of the sunrise, unexpected. He wasn't out to lose himself entirely on this rolling sea of grass. So he rode up atop a handy rise for a look-see all around, in hopes of spotting some distant landmark in such tricky light as there might be.

He couldn't see much. The moon wouldn't be rising for another hour or more and the Wyoming stars, while big and bright as diamonds, didn't shed enough light for him to make out the horizon, save as that part of the night where no stars shone. Then he looked twice at one faint twinkle just a tad further down in the distance than any other star. Then he muttered to his ponies, "Some damn fool has lit a fire over yonder. We'd best go see who it is."

Chapter 17

Nobody, red or white, would be dumb enough to kindle a campfire atop a rise with both Mister Lo and the U.S. Army on the prowl. Not knowing this for certain, Longarm tethered his ponies a quarter mile off in a low-slung willow clump, and did some serious pussyfooting with his Winchester cocked at port arms before he determined just what in thunder was burning over this way.

It was medicine. Coup sticks, feathered lances, feathered war bonnets, and shield covers smoldered atop more brightly burning cottonwood. Just outside the flickering red glow, atop the highest swell of the rise, other cottonwood had been selected with more care for a sky burial.

Indians seldom played tricks with their old-time religion. So Longarm drew gingerly close enough to make out all three blanket-wrapped forms atop the twig platform slung between the four stouter saplings selected in a nearby wooded draw. As he began to put it together, Longarm softly whistled and told the three dead Indians, "I'd say your medicine was piss-poor the other day as well. I was only sure about *one* of you. But of course, a boy can ride for some time and quite a ways with one bullet or more in him. When you ain't killed right out, unless you recover entirely, it's generally the second or third day you die."

He didn't like that fire nearby at all. Knowing anyone still keeping an eye on it would be even more surprised to see it suddenly go out, Longarm eased closer and reached up to take hold of some greasy trading-post wool as he softly explained, "I'm sorry, boys, I got to look you over just a mite."

He was even sorrier when he let the stink out of the bundle in the middle. That figured to be the one he'd shot just plain dead days ago in warm weather. One of the others was a tad bloated, but not too bad, while the last one they'd wrapped seemed pretty fresh. All three had been young, in their late teens or early twenties, before their pals had had to stick them up in the sky to destroy some of their own spoiled medicine as well.

As he re-wrapped the three of them, which seemed only right, Longarm muttered, "The way I read this, boys, your whole band carried their dead and wounded this far out from the Bozeman to do some serious rattle-shaking. They put you in the middle up here first, hoping you two on the outsides might make it, only you never did and so, as you died one after the other, they got mighty discouraged. Some older boys they'd been playing with must have sold them a bill of goods about strong medicine from the Shining Times. That'd account for the Pawnee war trophy, but would all of you boys be wearing dark blue Blackfoot moccasins if you were, say, Lakota or Cheyenne?"

As he covered the last dead Indian's pale face he grimaced and decided, "You likely wouldn't. I doubt if I'd want to wear the shoes of a dead man with no socks either. Moccasins don't fit worth a damn unless they're cut and sewn skintight. So all right, the three of you must be Blackfoot, only what are you doing in Lakota country and which way did your scared pals just go?"

He went back to his own ponies, swapped saddles, and gave them a little water and cracked corn before he fed himself a cheroot, explaining, "It's too early for me to break out any beans, but Lord only knows how far or how fast I might have to push you once I cut some damned sign. Meanwhile, we need more light to manage that, so eat up, and where's that damned moon this evening?"

It finally came up, nearly an hour later, and the difference made it worth the wait. For now that the prairie rolled silvery gray in the moonlight under a starry sky, you could separate the horizon from the land all around and, once he'd circled the dying embers and sky burial, leading his ponies afoot, only twice, he was able to find a fresh horse turd, as much by smell as by sight. Then, once he could hunker down and strike a match where a pony had been for certain and recently, he was able to read other signs, a crushed prairie flower here and a bent soapweed stem there, indicating the Indians had lit out to the east riding hard.

Longarm couldn't hope to overtake them on foot, or read enough sign to matter from the saddle, even riding slow. He followed slow but sure until he was sure of their heading, and then remounted, muttering, "They're steering on the sky and to hell with the weed clumps too. That means they'll likely stick to that same heading, due east, till dawn at least. But what's over that way any Siksika might want?"

He pressed on, trying to picture a mental map of the High Plains this far north. That was way easier than picturing Blackfoot headed for the Black Hills a tad to the left, ahead, or the Pine Ridge reserve a mite farther, to the right. He scowled at the starry eastern skyline and growled, "We're talking a long hard ride either way, and why would Blackfoot be bothering? Their own reserve up along the Front Range was high as near if they'd decided to quit whilst they were ahead."

That was a point to ponder as well. If they weren't intent on circling wide of their Absaroke enemies to the north, they could be headed for that Sun Dance the Lakota were fixing to hold whether the B.I.A. wanted them to or not.

Longarm decided either notion worked as well, and swung his mount south again, explaining, "We don't want to chase that many Indians anywheres when paid-up dragoons are headed this way to do it right. So now we'd best get all our asses to the telegraph office in Pumpkin Buttes and tell Matt Kincaid them young Blackfoot could be out to count coup at that big Lakota powwow!"

He knew Kincaid would bust a gut before he'd let a thing like that happen. For if the Blackfoot had ridden with the Lakota Confederacy in that last big rising, and if some came in counting coup with brand-new scalps, to stir up untested

146

warriors already excited by the self-inflicted pain around the Okipa pole . . .

"Let's go, ponies. We got us some ground to cover and some warning wires to send, *poco tiempo*!"

Chapter 18

Neither Deputy Larkin nor any of the other boys seemed surprised to see Longarm ride in the next morning, alive and well if somewhat tuckered. Nobody had told them he was supposed to be dead, bless their innocent hearts.

Ross Larkin caught up with Longarm in front of the Western Union as he was coming back out. Larkin nodded at the nearby tethered ponies and said, "Thought I recognized your rumps. How'd things go up by French Jenny's?"

Longarm offered his fellow lawman a smoke as he replied, "Just now wired my home office and the War Department. Before we set down so's I can tell you all about it, did you or did you not get Deacon Dunvegan's wire about them gunslicks who backshot a windmill drummer up yonder?"

Larkin nodded. "I did. They never come this way. Only new faces in town go with a railroad dick named MacNutt and his boys. The three of 'em come up from Douglas just yesterday. MacNutt says he knows you and that you can vouch for him, by the way. I had to ask who the three of 'em might be, even though nobody in the party fit old Deacon's frantic wire."

Longarm said, "It so happens I do know Hamish MacNutt. Him and me foiled a train robbery one time. But has the railroad

148

started up again, before the army could even get here?"

Larkin lit both their smokes. "Not hardly. MacNutt says his job is to make sure it's safe before they send any trains along the tracks. They don't mean to try before the army assures 'em about them Indians. Come on, we can ask 'em about it if you like. The three of 'em were having breakfast at the Elkhorn just now."

Longarm hesitated, decided the two ponies were all right where they were, and tagged along with Larkin. In a town that size they didn't have far to go, and as they stepped inside the saloon Longarm saw that, sure enough, that railroad dick he remembered so fondly was seated at a corner table with two other galoots Longarm didn't recognize. All three were wearing mail-order suits. So things might have gone way smoother than they did had not one of them screamed, loud as a schoolmarm with a mouse running up her leg, "Great balls of fire, it's that son-of-a-bitching Longarm! Alive!"

So Longarm was going for his gun at about the same time, but it might have gone bad for him had not Ross Larkin slapped leather at the same time, making it two against three as all concerned blazed away at once!

But while the one who said he was Hamish MacNutt aimed straight at Longarm, his aim was a mite off as he pulled the trigger, for it's hard to concentrate with a round of .44-40 smack between your eyes and your brains blown all over a plaster wall.

Ross Larkin dropped the one who'd evoked Longarm's name in vain, while Longarm killed the other, knowing he had to be the killer who'd backshot poor old Underwood by mistake.

But Larkin hadn't been with him to French Jenny's and back and so, as they found themselves still on their feet in a blue haze of gunsmoke, Larkin exclaimed, "That was sure close. Why did we just have to do that, pard?"

Longarm began to reload as he soberly replied, "I'm still working on it. Both the one calling himself MacNutt and that pants-pisser who yelled my name knew me on sight. That leaves the one you nailed as the killer who backshot a windmill drummer he took for me."

Larkin ejected his own spent brass. "All right. Say him and

one other holding their getaway ponies at the telegraph office rid around us, changed duds, and backtracked with MacNutt aboard his buckboard, things still read mighty fuzzy. MacNutt just told us you and him were pals and that you could vouch for him, Uncle Sam!"

Longarm smiled thinly and explained, "He thought I was dead, leaving him free to say I'd sucked his pecker, did it suit his plans. The hell of it was that until just now I really had him down as a reasonably honest Pinkerton man. I reckon we live and learn."

By now the barkeep had crawled the length of his duckboards behind the bar on his hands and knees, to peer out around one end, ashen-faced but somewhat recovered as he asked if it was over and if there was anything he could do to help.

Larkin told him to get over to the front entrance and tell anyone outside to stay there for now. As the barkeep rose to assure them a few more minutes, Larkin turned back to Longarm and demanded, "Learn what? Was the sneaky son of a bitch working for Pinkerton or what?"

Longarm replied, "Got to send some more wires before I'll feel free to bet a month's pay on it. But try her this way. Pinkerton wired me they had a MacNutt riding the rails back and forth. That's what he seemed to be doing when first we met and I thought we were foiling a train robbery together. But look how it works if this rascal switched places with the real MacNutt. Say he recognized me, knew about some other railroad jobs I'd worked on in the past, and suspected I was neither working alone nor as dumb as I was talking. The Brothers Plimmons were really dumb. They were waiting just up the line to rob the train whilst the fake railroad dicks on board tried in vain to stop 'em."

Larkin had an imagination too. He whistled and said, "Shooting his less reliable confederates before you and anyone working with you could capture them in a more conversational condition would have been about what the Reno or James boys would have doubtless felt *they* had to do. But after you bought his whole flimflam and went on after Blackfoot, why did they try to gun you as well? Revenge?"

Longarm shook his head and said, "I just said I got to send

150

me some wires if I'm ever to tie up all the loose ends. Until somebody tells me different, though, I'm going with a sort of bedroom farce with a would-be mastermind suspecting me of screwing his wife when all the time I was after the upstairs maid."

Then he headed for the doorway. Larkin wasn't about to be left in the air like that. So he tagged along, asking what in thunder Longarm was talking about.

As they parted the batwings to find the plank walk crowded with curious folk, Larkin nodded at two cowhands he was used to ordering around and said, "I want them three dead boys in yonder tidied up and displayed on cellar doors or whatever for everyone to see, with a view to someone recognizing at least one of 'em. They don't seem to have been who they said they was. I'll be with this federal rider here should anything interesting occur."

Longarm had already started walking. Larkin caught up, saying, "If this was my case and mine alone, I'd likely move slower and surer. You didn't even give me time to pat them bodies down for identification, but you just now said you was anxious to find out who they might have been!"

Longarm kept going, explaining, "They'd already gone to some trouble pretending to be somebody else. Nobody on our wanted lists is likely to pack his own birth certificate about. Whether their leader's packing the Pinkerton credentials of the real Hamish MacNutt or not is neither here nor there. He describes sort of average, when you don't look close. Pinkerton's already assured me their one and original Hamish Pinkerton was thirty-seven years old, five-foot-ten with an average build, and so on. Now I got to ask 'em if their man ever had all his teeth pulled. It ain't easy to spot a good set of false teeth unless a man's lying dead with his mouth agape and his jaw hanging nice and slack."

Larkin grimaced and said he hadn't noticed that about the apparent leader back yonder. Longarm said, "I'm pretty sure he was their straw boss, up this way at least. I'm still working on whether he'd been trying to run the operation from Denver, and come out in the open to do things right after hearing, premature, I was out of the picture."

By the time they got back to the Western Union office

Longarm had decided the treacherous one calling himself MacNutt had wired ahead to other business associates, who'd wound up getting run over by those Indians, bless their red hides, before they could carry out their orders. So two more, including one with the nerve but not the know-how to recognize their intended victim, had tracked down poor Underwood by casually asking along the trail about a pal in a suit and mustache, riding a bay with a McClellan saddle.

Going up the Western Union steps, Longarm explained, "Once they wired their pal down by the Denver railroad depot I was dead, he beelined back, by rail a good part of the way, to get back in the train-robbing business, see?"

Larkin frowned. "Not hardly. The damned old trains ain't running. They won't be running before the army tidies up this Indian scare. So how in blue blazes could they have been planning to rob any trains?"

Longarm sighed. "There's nothing like getting in on the ground floor. Enough dragoons to do the job on Mister Lo are on their way even as we speak, and would you like to hazard a guess as to how much cash or postal money orders the first few baggage cars will be packing after all this service starts up again?"

Larkin whistled and said, "Holy shit! I'm waiting on some spring veal checks my ownself, and them sneaks we just shot up just proved how good they were at pretending to be someone else. I'm glad we shot 'em before they cashed my veal checks, the thieving sons of bitches!"

By this time they were inside. So Longarm advised Larkin to hush while he blocked out telegrams to the Pinkertons, Billy Vail, and as long as he was at it, the War Department. Every little bit helped when you were trying to track Horse Indians across range baking harder and drier by each sunrise.

After that, Longarm had little to prevent him from tending to less important but still vital chores while he waited for some replies to his wires.

Pretty little Elsa Stern seemed friendly as ever, whether he'd laid her in the dark or not, when he paid a call on her to let her know her stock was all right and that she couldn't have it back just yet. As he handed her more cash he explained how,

152

whether his boss wanted him back or not, he still had to get down to his own saddle and a railroad ride at Douglas. She invited him inside and fed him some buttermilk and marble cake while they worked out the way they could get the livery in Douglas to get her two bays back to her. As they did so Longarm kept watching for some sign from her that this conversation might be going a bit too formal, considering. But while a body movement here and a fleeting Mona Lisa expression there made him *hope* that had been her in the dark that time, it was up to her if she wanted to slip into something more comfortable than that thin summer frock. But she was still acting innocent by the time he'd finished his second glass of buttermilk, and so, none of the other suspects being around to question, and no federal crime being involved in any case, he felt obliged to get back to his feet, tick his hat brim to her, and be on his way.

Was he imagining it, or did she look sort of wistful when he told her he'd likely be riding on once he got some answers to his wires? She for certain busted something on her kitchen floor as the screen door slammed behind him.

He didn't look back. It was her china to bust or not bust as she might choose. He didn't know why women did that. He did know that the one time he'd gone back to ask, a fool redhead had busted a damned old platter over his poor skull.

He knew it was still early, so he headed back to the Elkhorn to see what anyone else might have to say. There was quite a crowd out front, for such a small town. It sure beat all how curious folks were about gents they might not look at twice alive once they were dead.

So far, nobody in Pumpkin Buttes had owned up to knowing the nondescript cadavers propped up on sloped pine planks near the doorway of the saloon, which was now much busier. One of those hands Larkin had ordered about before sidled up to Longarm and said Larkin was inside, adding, "We got out their wallets. All three packed voter registration cards giving Denver addresses and sort of bland last names, in Larkin's opinion. He said you might be interested to know the one calling his fool self a Pinkerton man named MacNutt registered to vote in Colorado as a John Green. Not a thing on him to intimate

153

he'd ever worked for the Pinks. He must have had a heap of brass."

Longarm shrugged. "That's what you have to have when you don't have nothing better. I'm still waiting to find out whether he killed the real MacNutt and switched places with him, or just used the name of a real Pink working some other train. I like that better."

The hand grinned and said, "I reckon the real MacNutt would too. But speaking of brass—"

"He'd have had to have had some either way." Longarm explained. "He must have been sweating bullets till he got the word I'd been backshot. He knew that even though I'd been dumb enough to buy his story once, I'd be sure to think twice once a train the Pinks were supposed to be guarding got robbed, better, just up the line. Worse yet for him, I'd know him on sight, no matter who he wanted to say he was, the next time we met."

The hand nodded at the dead man they were jawing about as he said, "I'd like more privacy if I were setting up train robberies too."

Then somebody else remarked on how peaceful all three of the dead villains looked, and so Longarm turned away before the asshole could say they looked like they were asleep.

He got the sweet aftertaste of that marble cake out of his mouth with the needed beer he felt he deserved about now. But the saloon was crowded, and it soon got tedious having total strangers slap him on the back and ask questions he didn't have all the answers to yet. So after he'd watched the wall clock over the silent piano a desperate spell, he ducked out to see how good Western Union's service was.

As he strode down the shady side of the dusty street he spied a haze of dust with a fluttering army guidon imbedded in it coming at him the other way. He got up the nearest wooden stairs to keep his head above the really thick dust as the dusty dragoons riding column-of-fours trotted past, poor bastards. He'd ridden a time or more with Captain Matt Kincaid, and so he knew the whalebone-and-rawhide regular had made such good time by subjecting his command to that mile-eating but ball-busting pace all the way.

Longarm couldn't make out any faces in that haze of dry

prairie loam and horseshit. So he strode on to the telegraph office.

Billy Vail hadn't heard he was dead. He was simply vexed about his deleted-by-Western-Union deputy neglecting to keep in touch, and wanted him back in Denver deleted by Western Union.

The Pinkerton Detective Agency assured him their Hamish MacNutt had all or almost all his own teeth. They further agreed, on more careful consideration of their own damn files at last, that MacNutt had been on duty somewhere between Colorado Springs and El Paso at the time the Brothers Plimmons had met up with Longarm and whoever that other MacNutt had really been.

The War Department in Washington hadn't gotten around to answering yet. Longarm was not surprised. He knew Billy Vail was expecting an answer from him. So he wrote he was still tying up some loose ends. The attempted assassination of a federal deputy with a view to robbing the U.S. mails had to be a federal matter no matter how Billy felt about Indian policy.

Then, as long as he was there, he sent some other questions out on the wire, explaining to the bemused Western Union clerk, "Have you ever asked one question only to find the answer inspired still more questions?"

The clerk said, "Nope, but my wife's sure good at that." Then he got right back to his telegraph set. So Longarm strode back outside, lighting a fresh cheroot. That was when he met up with Captain Matt Kincaid of the U.S. Dragoons.

The somewhat more refined-looking but hard-as-nails officer was considered handsome when he was smooth-shaven and less dusty. As they shook out front Longarm said, "I should have known you'd want to wire your headquarters as soon as you and your boys arrived, Matt. I'll go back inside with you and ask the clerk to set the messages I just writ aside."

But Kincaid said, "No need to, Custis." He drew a folded note from the cuff of one buckskin gauntlet, explaining, "They can put this on the wire anytime this afternoon. Wrote it on the trail. Stock message assuring the old man we're making good time and following the usual orders."

Longarm walked inside with him, anyway asking, "What

155

usual orders are we jawing about, Matt? I doubt you'll find shit if you just push on up the Bozeman Trail with your patrols out to either side the usual few miles. You see—"

"In a minute," Kincaid told him as the clerk came to the counter. The army man handed over his message and said, "I'd like this to go to G.H.Q. Fort Laramie, collect, whenever you have time."

The clerk said he'd get it off within, say, a quarter hour. Kincaid thanked him and, turning back to Longarm, suggested, "Let's wet our whistles while we talk over old times and more serious Indian fighting. My boys and me have to be riding on, but there's surely time for a drink while we compare notes."

Longarm nodded. "Let's go anywheres but the Elkhorn then. By now your dragoons will have noticed the most popular saloon in town as well, and it was crowded enough when I just left it."

Kincaid said Longarm knew the town better than he did. Longarm proved it by steering them to a hole-in-the-wall boozery he'd noticed more than once in his travels. It was small but empty. The old bald buzzard dozing behind the bar was so glad to see them he said the first round was on the house, adding, "What on earth's going on down by the Elkhorn? Have they struck gold or discovered the Fountain of Youth in one of the spittoons?"

They both listened with interest as Longarm brought them up to date on the shootout in a rival saloon. The old-timer running this one complained, "I wish someone would commit murder, sodomy, or rape down *this* way. At the rate things are going I'm going to have to commit arson. I used to have a bulldog with a drinking problem, and the boys used to enjoy buying him drinks and watching him get drunk. But then he died. Drinking too much will do that to you, you know."

His two customers agreed moderation in all vices was the best policy. Then the army man ordered the next round and held up his shot glass with a thin smile, saying, "To Mister Lo, or let's make that to Mister Red Cloud of the Oglala Lakota in honor of a real soldier."

Longarm clinked with him, saying, "I'll drink to that. No battle commander, red or white, could say they were any smarter

156

than old Red Cloud, the only Horse Indian who ever fought the U.S. Army to a draw."

Kincaid grimaced. "Let's not get sickening about it. He got a truce out of us and a temporary peace treaty out of Washington. We never admitted defeat back in '68."

Longarm smiled wryly. "Neither did Red Cloud. He thought that treaty gave him and his people the Black Hills for keeps. But let's not rake them ashes over. Last I heard of Red Cloud he was alive and well, over to the Pine Ridge Agency, being he was too smart to come out that last time, when Custer lost his hair and Washington lost its temper and gave up treating with Indian nations as if they was nations. I was trying to tell you about them Siksika when you stopped me at the Western Union just now."

Kincaid frowned and demanded, "What's a Siksika? They've sent us out after Blackfoot."

So Longarm said, "Sorry, I thought you knew the so-called Blackfoot called themselves Siksika. But come to study on it, them Blackfoot riding with the Lakota would be known as Siha Sapa to their Lakota-speaking allies."

Kincaid looked relieved. "Oh, sure, you mean the Siha Sapa up around Little Bighorn that time. That's how we have 'em in our order-of-battle manual."

"You boys are both wrong," the old barkeep chimed in, smiling smugly as he added, "I was out here in the beaver trade when a man could sure get hurt guessing wrong about feathers and paint. The boys you describe as Siksika and Siha Sapa ain't the same sort of Indians at all."

The two younger men, both experienced Indian fighters, exchanged wary glances. Because they were experienced, Longarm said, "Well, I could be as confused as the army order-of-battle books, but don't Siha Sapa mean Foot and Black or Blue, literally, and ain't the Siksika the ones everyone calls Blackfoot Indians?"

The old erstwhile mountain man nodded but explained, "Your Piegans, Bloods, and other Siksika are Algonquin talkers, related to the Cree. The Siha Sapa, or *Blackfoot Sioux,* are a Lakota *warrior society* as likes to wear dark moccasins for some fool reason. I know lots of folk mix the two kinds of Indians up. I've had this conversation before. During that last big fuss along the Little Bighorn I won me a heap of bar bets. The Blackfoot fighting us that summer were Blackfoot-Sioux, not Blackfoot-Blackfoot. I'll bet on that, offering ten to one. Any takers?"

There weren't any. Both Longarm and Kincaid knew how easy it was to guess wrong about Indians. Kincaid said, "I'd better check that again with the B.I.A."

Longarm said, "I can tell you what they'll tell you. They told me and Billy Vail the Indians raiding up and down the Bozeman Trail right now are Blackfoot, period, off a reserve or reserves unknown. Real Blackfoot, though I have been assured more than once no Siksika are on the warpath this spring. Meanwhile, the same B.I.A. who's so casual about tribal affiliations has been bitching about an unauthorized Sun Dance their Lakota, not their Siksika, have been whispering about. So add it up."

Kincaid finished his drink before he replied with a sigh, "Ours not to reason why or change orders in the field without a hell of a lot more than that to go on! No matter who's been up to what, I mean to scout along the Bozeman at least as far north as the Bighorn Crow Agency. I'd sure like to have you riding point for us again, Custis."

Longarm shrugged. "It was always fun. But not this time, Matt. To begin with, Billy Vail's ordered me not to. He must have known you boys would get lost hunting Mister Lo again. I'll allow my first intent was to nip this Indian shit in the bud before anyone got hurt. But one man can only do so much when assholes are bound and determined to get hurt. So I'd best be on my way."

Kincaid growled, "Thanks. Which of us did you just decribe as assholes out to get hurt, you fucking feather merchant?"

Longarm chuckled fondly and said, "Don't get your bowels in an uproar, soldier boy. I meant the Indians. The ones I've seen so far looked like kids too young to have counted coup on Custer. I know you and your dragoons are only out to do your job. There ought to be a way to leave women, children, and horses out of Indian warfare, but there ain't and nobody's paying me to be a sentimental fool. You say you'll only be patrolling as far north as the Crow agency, Matt?"

Kincaid nodded. "Until I get further orders. Why do you ask if you don't want to ride with us?"

Longarm said, "Wanted to make sure my Siksika pals were safe from any Sand Creek or Washita-type misunderstandings. It's been nice talking to you, Matt. Now I got to get it on down the road. I'm commencing to understand things better."

Chapter 19

He Whose Brow Glows Red like Sunset Clouds and so forth, better known to his people as Mahpiua Luta, or as Red Cloud to the Wasichu, was a no longer young but still virile giant who sort of looked the way Abe Lincoln might have looked if his folks had been Indians. As a war chief who'd fought the U.S. Army to a standstill, twice, and then been smart enough to stay out of the dumb moves by both sides leading up to Little Bighorn, Red Cloud rated his own spacious cabin and other handsome handouts to assure his continued life of peaceable ease at the Pine Ridge Agency—or Wazi Ahanahan, as he prefered to call it.

Red Cloud had been born smart, and his years spent at tribal politics and cavalry maneuvers had honed his native intelligence. So Red Cloud felt troubled, troubled, when some young men told him his good enemy and old friend Longarm had ridden in alone and wanted to meet with him before he'd even paid the usual courtesy call on the Wasichu agent over near Wounded Knee.

The sun hung low in the west, in a sky of blood, when Red Cloud stepped out on his plank porch to greet the tall deputy and the others buzzing around him like horn flies searching for a wound to lay their eggs in. Most of them were just young men from the Siha Sapa Society. Red Cloud knew he could handle them. But there was that unruly Shunka Gleska, with his arrogant face painted as if he had the smallpox, or taken many scalps, many, even though he'd been too young to take part in the Custer Fight, and even though there hadn't been many good fights since.

As they got to Red Cloud's porch steps, Shunka Gleska held up Longarm's .44-40, announcing in English lest his brag not have the full audience he felt it deserved, "Do not be afraid of this one, Grandfather. I told him he could not get any closer to you unless he gave me his gun."

Longarm muttered, "Hold on, now, Spotted Dog. I said you could hold it for me whilst I powwowed with your chief. I never said it was yours for keeps."

Red Cloud tried not to smile as he wondered whether Shunka Gleska had ever heard of those derringers half the Wasichu carried in their vest pockets. There were so many things about the Wasichu to keep in mind and these boys were so young. The old warrior nodded and said, "I think we ought to go inside, sit down, and talk."

Longarm said that was what he'd ridden one hell of a ways just to do. Inside the clean but sparsely furnished cabin one of Red Cloud's women had already spread a blanket, a good one, on the plank flooring with its corners carefully lined up with the four Good Directions. Then, being a woman, she'd lit out the back door to scout for herbs or whatever Lakota women did when their men were talking.

Only the arrogantly painted and blue-shod Shunka Gleska felt important enough to sit right on the blanket with Red Cloud and Longarm. The others hunkered against the cabins walls, their own dark moccasins clear of the cream-colored Hudson Bay wool.

It was Red Cloud's cabin as well as his blanket. So nobody was supposed to say anything before Red Cloud had his own say. They all watched, silently, as Red Cloud gravely produced a medicine bundle painted long ago in the old vegetable dye colors. But when Red Cloud drew forth a calumet with a real stone bowl and real bear claws from a real bear, or prairie grizzly, Shunka Gleska just had to protest. "This Wasichu is an enemy who owes us blood for blood, Grandfather! Hear us, he is the one who killed three of our brothers over near the Powder River. He admitted this, just now, as we were bringing him to you for judgment—not to *smoke* with, you old fool!"

Everyone there but Red Cloud and the sassy Spotted Dog had to suck in his breath a mite at that deadly insult. The kid hadn't called his elder a sister-fucker or a coward yet, but you just didn't call any Lakota a fool unless you were prepared to prove you were a whole lot smarter.

Red Cloud knew that. He went on packing the pipe bowl with tobacco and shredded cherry bark as he softly remarked, "I have yet to say I want to smoke with anyone. When you get to be my age, if you ever do, you might like to get ready, ahead of time, for anything. I would like to hear more about your great pony raid, and how you lost three young men while bringing back two scalps and less than ten new ponies. You say it was this one Wasichu, by himself, who counted coup on Mato Napin, Tatoke Ska, and Wanigi Witco, driving all of you who lived away?"

Longarm murmured, modestly, "I had a Crow gal with me, Chief."

Red Cloud just stared at the younger painted and self-appointed war leader, as if he expected something mighty good. Shunka Gleska said something dreadful in his own lingo, but remembered they had a guest in time to protest, "He had medicine, powerful medicine. He didn't drop all three of them with his medicine rifle. Just Wanigi Witco, in spite of his ghost signs that were supposed to turn aside anything but medicine bullets. The other two died later, of small wounds that shouldn't have killed a woman. That is why we wouldn't let him any closer to you with his guns. We think he puts something on his bullets."

Red Cloud cocked an eyebrow at Longarm, who said, innocently, "I find mutton grease is good for keeping one's ammo good in damp weather. Ain't got nothing but the factory wax on anything right now."

Then he pointed at one pockmarked kid hunkered in a far corner to add, "I'd like to say a word about that boy yonder, Red Cloud. When I spilt Crazy Ghost, just like Spotted Dog said, fair and square with a plain old Winchester .44-40 lead,

162

that kid was the one who rode into easy range of my gun sights to carry his dead comrade from the field."

The Indian kid blushed like a gal who'd just won a cake-bake as Red Cloud nodded and said, "*Wa heya*, a man who would do a thing like that would be entitled to one feather, plain, but worn straight up."

Shunka Gleska pointed Longarm's sixgun at Longarm, demanding, "What would you award *me* for killing the man who killed the man this other hero picked up dead?"

Red Cloud said, "Nothing. That would be a woman-hearted way to kill anybody. We are Oglala Lakota, not Pawnee, Shunka Gleska. Longarm has come here, alone, to say something. I do not think he could be here to count coup on young men who should have known better. I am waiting to hear what this Wasichu who fights good and talks straight has to say."

So Longarm said, "I rode in alone because I wanted to get here first, not because I am the only rider who might be headed this way. I see you already know about this asshole and some other kids going out to bust windows and steal apples without permission from their elders. You know me to be a live-and-let-live cuss, Red Cloud. Seeing the kids got safely home, with the score about even, I'd be willing to settle for just recovering them stolen ponies and arresting this one troublemaker here."

Shunka Gleska cocked Longarm's sixgun, mistaking it for a single-action thumb-buster, the ignorant asshole. Red Cloud shot the younger Indian a warning look and told Longarm, "I don't think I want you to do that. I know these young men have been foolish. I know the Great Father says Oglala who kill Wasichu deserve to hang. Maybe they do. I can let you have the ponies they brought back with them. I can say I don't want revenge for the three young men who got themselves killed by acting foolish in times of peace. But if I let you arrest this boy and turn him over to your hangmen, I will lose all the power I still have over my people, all!"

Longarm nodded soberly and replied, "I knew when I rode in I was giving you a hard row to hoe, Chief. But I got my own rows to hoe, and I can only bend the laws of the land so much. U.S. citizens of the paler persuasion have been murdered by Indians. At least one of their victims was a decent old cuss too. You might or might not be able to stop me. Anyone can see this sneering son of a bitch has the drop on me. Meanwhile, there's a column of dragoons out hunting this old boy and all his kissing cousins as well. The government's heard about that big Sun Dance prayer meeting you've been planning, Red Cloud, so all in all, this would be one hell of a time for you to murder a guest under your own roof."

Red Cloud sat there with the unlit calumet in his lap, looking as if he didn't know whether to shit or go blind as he almost whimpered, "Hear me, this is getting out of hand! I never told these young men to get in trouble. I don't even belong to the Siha Sapa Society! I know nothing, nothing about that Okipa that damned Tatanka Yatanka has announced. He's been nothing but trouble, trouble, since he came back down from Canada after the Custer Fight. Nobody listens to me anymore, nobody! Hear me, I got good terms for us after I beat the blue sleeves and burned their forts along the Bozeman Trail. I told them what would happen when they wanted to fight some more in the Summer of Greasy Grass. Why do they keep listening to untried leaders like Tatanka Yatanka and this child, Shunka Gleska?"

Longarm ignored the .44-40 trained right at his ear as he told Red Cloud, "If it's any comfort to you, Sitting Bull tells me he can't get anyone to listen to *him* since he come down from Canada and signed up for his own B.I.A. room and board. I'm fixing to take your word you had nothing to do with the recent foolishness over to the Powder River country. You might want to advise Sitting Bull he'd best pull in his horns and take Buffalo Bill Cody up on that offer to tour with that Wild West show. Meanwhile, seeing you just admitted you've no control over Spotted Dog here, I won't ask you to surrender him to me officially."

Then he turned to the Indian holding a gun on him to calmly add, "I'd like my side arm back now, Spotted Dog. As of now you are under arrest for murder, inciting to riot, and hell, that ought to be enough to run you in, old son."

The Indian pulled the trigger. The detonation in such a confined space was deafening. Longarm had been braced for it, and he still winced and covered both ears with his hands, too late.

164

The Indians were even more surprised to see how it had turned out. For Longarm had known what he was doing when he'd paused by a prairie water hole early that morning to stuff his gun barrel chock full of 'dobe mud, knowing where he was headed, how things might turn out, and how solid 'dobe could dry out in a whole afternoon.

He'd loosened a few strategic screws too. So while it was a shame what he'd done to his poor old gun, Colt turned out the same model .44-40 at reasonable cost, and there lay the unreasonable Spotted Dog with a shattered pistol still held in a death grip and his head and shoulders all torn to hell by bits and pieces of a gun with nowhere to blow but back.

It looked worse as the smoke started to clear, so that was doubtless why the other young Indians lit out before the last of the smoke had completely cleared. Red Cloud seemed made of sterner stuff. So as the tough old bird lit his calumet at last, Longarm quietly asked, "Was that *wakan-wakan* stuff they was yelling about the great medicine I must have, Chief?"

Red Cloud smiled thinly and said, "They think you must be Okihadi, the really *bad* medicine. I don't know what you are, Longarm. But now I think we should smoke together. There are men I like to have as enemies and there are men I would rather have as friends. Do you want to be my friend, Longarm?"

The younger fighting man left in the blood-spattered cabin took the calumet gravely, saying, "Damned right. You're a pretty frightening cuss in your own right, Red Cloud."

Chapter 20

President Hayes and his prissy First Lady, Lemonade Lucy, seemed too cheap to serve decent liquor at the White House. So in the end the War Department was just as glad to be spared the expenses of a summer campaign.

The Bureau of Indians Affairs was even more pleased by the peace and quiet at Pine Ridge occasioned by Longarm's rough justice. By tricking the troublemaking Blackfoot-Sioux into a shameful death at his own hands, Longarm had convinced a heap of other sore losers that Wakan Tanka just wasn't ready for another rising yet.

Longarm picked up a fresh .44-40 at the first stop off the reservation, and had a gunsmith in Douglas rework the barrel and grips for as sudden a draw as ever while he picked up his trusty McClellan and made arrangements to get Elsa Stern's ponies back to her. That still left him time, before his south-bound train left for Denver, to send some tidy-up wires and pick up some magazines to read along the way.

So they were naturally expecting him at Marshal Vail's office, and when he failed to show up, hours after his train had arrived and then an added hour after lunch, Billy Vail sent young Henry, the kid who played the typewriter out front, to track him down.

Henry was no tracker. But he had the common sense to commence at the beginning, and so, sure enough, he caught up with Longarm at the Union Depot consuming a cheroot and reading a copy of the *Police Gazette* out on the platform, seated on a shipping crate.

Henry had on a better suit, and the crate looked a mite too small as well as splintery. So Henry just braced one instep on a corner of Longarm's chosen seat as he quietly observed, "Marshal Vail was sort of wondering if you still worked for him and the taxpayers of these United States. What am I supposed to tell him when or if I go back to the office without you?"

Longarm set his magazine aside, saying, "We'll all go together, like the old song says, as soon as the north bound I'm waiting on gets here. You know I like to tie up all the loose strings I can before you have to retype my final report in triplicate, Henry."

The clerk-typist frowned down at him. "I've already filed that fairly complete night letter you wired in from Wounded Knee. Are you saying you left something out?"

"Not about Indians or even mean whites I brushed with up yonder," Longarm assured him, before smiling indulgently as the gun grips peeking out from under the prissy clerk's frock coat and asking, "How come you're so armed and dangerous this afternoon, Henry?"

To which the clerk primly replied, "The boss sends me looking for an overdue deputy with your rep unarmed? Surely you jest. But never mind what I'm doing here with a gun, Longarm. What are *you* doing here with . . . where's your Winchester?"

Longarm patted Henry's coattail, saying, "In the check room with my saddle and possibles, of course. I doubt I'll even need to pistol-whup the son of a bitch I'm waiting for. He's too sly a crook to risk a go-for-broke when all I can hang on him is criminal conspiracy, if that."

Henry knew Longarm well enough to consider the general tone of that report he'd just typed in triplicate before he said, "I give up. You killed four Indians, and all those would-be train robbers mucking up your mission would seem to be accounted for, so who's left?"

Longarm cocked his head and got to his feet, saying, "Train's coming. The real Hamish MacNutt's been riding it back and forth betwixt Douglas and El Paso all this time. Pinkerton tells me he lives here in town with an otherwise innocent gal. I figure it would distress her less if I arrested him here, as he gets off the train."

Henry smiled uncertainly and said, "I'm sure it would. But how can you arrest the real MacNutt after gunning the master crook who was just impersonating him, up the other way entirely?"

Longarm smiled wolfishly with the cheroot gripped between his bared teeth at a jaunty angle as he replied. "To tidy up, like I said. The one calling himself Green when he wasn't pretending to be MacNutt turned out, on closer examination, to be another Denver resident and erstwhile licensed guard called Burke, David W. Burke. Don't ever get tattoed or wounded in a war before you apply for a state license if you don't want anyone to ever figure out who you used to be, Henry."

The clerk grimaced. "I know, I know, the other two were known crooks with long but petty records I saw no need to include in the final report. Get to why we're arresting Hamish MacNutt for being victimized by a brazen liar called Burke."

Longarm said, "Because Burke lied so brazen, of course. My first thought was that they'd done something mean to the real Pink so's they could replace 'em with Burke. When his agency assured me he was still alive and well, with what seemed an airtight alibi, I had to study on that alibi. The first thing I noticed was that unless we're talking about a French bedroom farce, it's just too damned easy for real folks to trip over one another unless they've agreed, in advance, not to."

Henry blinked and said, "I see what you mean. But how are you ever going to prove a real railroad dick gave a crook permission, and mayhaps some coaching, to impersonate him?"

Longarm moved closer to the platform edge, staring down the tracks at the approaching smoke plume of the northbound flier, as he explained, "That's the easy part. Remember that bounty money posted on the Brothers Plimmons?"

Henry nodded. "Of course, but I don't see how anyone just claiming to be the railroad dick who nailed them could file for a dime without . . . Oh, no, the real MacNutt couldn't have been *that* dumb!"

"He waited till his pals wired him I'd been backshot," Longarm explained. "He gave a lame excuse about not having been on his usual rounds that particular day, and till I got others to sort of wondering, lame was good enough. Money was the root of all this evil, and so that was still another motive they had to murder me. I just can't wait to hear MacNutt's explanations when he ought to discover, for the very first time, I was still alive when he modesty came forward to collect the rewards on those train robbers his alter ego and me put out of business!"

Henry said he wanted to hear it too. Longarm wasn't piggy about others sharing credit for an arrest. That was why he'd already been able to post a copper badge from the Denver P.D. at each end of the platform. He told Henry, "All right. He'll likely ride in aboard the express car, just behind the tender. He's paid to act like he's guarding the safe with his life, the two-faced prick. So you and me had best be by yonder awning post when she rolls to a stop."

Henry didn't argue. He tagged along with some admiration as, just about the time they reached the post Longarm had indicated, the locomotive and tender rolled past, slow, and the train came to a hissing halt with the big side door of the express car staring right down at them.

When it failed to open right off, Longarm moved over to tap on it with his new .44-40. The door slid right open. When Longarm asked the baggage clerk staring down at them where their security man was, the railroader replied, "Search me. Old Hamish drifted off somewheres as we were rolling into the yards. You might try the dining car."

Longarm glanced dubiously along the now-crowded platform. Then Henry yelled, "No! Don't!" in a prissy voice as he drew his own sixgun and fired it—manly enough, as things turned out.

For even as Longarm spun around, his own gun trained north on general principles, a nondescript but neatly suited stranger who'd been aiming at Longarm's back from atop the coal in the tender landed on his head up the platform with a sickening crunch.

His gun, like his pearl-gray Stetson, landed nowhere near him. So Longarm only took a couple of thoughtful steps as he saw a blue-uniformed roundsman coming faster from the

169

north and an ashen-faced engineer peered down from the cab of his locomotive to call out, "In the name of God, that was our Pinkerton man, you damned fools!"

Longarm told him to shut up, turned soberly to Henry, and said, "That was mighty sweet of you, old son. Aside from saving my life, you likely saved us both a heap of paperwork. I don't know how we'd have ever convicted such a devious bastard if he hadn't found out I was alive after all and decided to end this game of blindman's bluff once and for all."

Henry sighed and said, "It's what you get for sending so many wires all up and down the line, and I'm glad it's over too. But I've really got to stop finding you for Marshal Vail, Longarm. I'm starting to get as wild a reputation as you and—"

"That reminds me," Longarm said. "We can't go back to the office till we settle accounts down here with the Denver P.D. and the coroner. So seeing the day's already almost shot, and seeing there's this new barmaid at the Black Cat who just come out West and admires us Wild Westerners . . ."

"I don't know." Henry said. "How do you know she'll have a pretty friend for me?"

Longarm replied with a laugh, "Hell, who did you think I meant to introduce her to, you ferocious buckaroo? I told you she was new in town because a gal who's been here longer told me she'd just arrived and didn't have nobody yet. She's the pretty friend the one I already *got* has been trying to fix up with another old cowhand, see?"

Henry saw, but had to sheepishy allow he didn't know if he could pass for an old cowhand. So Longarm said soothingly, "Don't worry. I told you she was from back East. If she can pass for innocent you can likely pass for cow."

Henry gulped and asked, "You mean you're fixing me up with . . . a sure thing, you randy rascal?"

To which Longarm could only modestly reply, "Sure I am, stud. Would you fix up a man who'd just saved your life with anything less?"

Watch for

LONGARM AND THE GOLD HUNTERS

153rd in the bold LONGARM series
from Jove

Coming in September!

GILES TIPPETTE

Author of the best-selling WILSON YOUNG
SERIES, BAD NEWS, and CROSS FIRE

is back with his most exciting
Western adventure yet!

JAILBREAK

Time is running out for Justa Williams, owner of the Half-
Moon Ranch in West Texas. His brother Norris is being held in
a Mexican jail, and neither bribes nor threats can free him.

Now, with the help of a dozen kill-crazy Mexican *banditos*,
Justa aims to blast Norris out. But the worst is yet to come:
a hundred-mile chase across the Mexican desert with fifty
federales in hot pursuit.

The odds of reaching the Texas border are a million to nothing . . . and if the Williams brothers don't watch their backs,
the road to freedom could turn into the road to hell!

Turn the page for an exciting preview of
JAILBREAK by Giles Tippette

On sale now, wherever Jove Books are sold!

At supper Norris, my middle brother, said, "I think we got some trouble on that five-thousand acres down on the border near Laredo."

He said it serious, which is the way Norris generally says everything. I quit wrestling with the steak Buttercup, our cook, had turned into rawhide and said, "What are you talking about? How could we have trouble on land lying idle?"

He said, "I got word from town this afternoon that a telegram had come in from a friend of ours down there. He says we got some kind of squatters taking up residence on the place."

My youngest brother, Ben, put his fork down and said, incredulously, "*That* five-thousand acres? Hell, it ain't nothing but rocks and cactus and sand. Why in hell would anyone want to squat on that worthless piece of nothing?"

Norris just shook his head. "I don't know. But that's what the telegram said. Came from Jack Cole. And if anyone ought to know what's going on down there it would be him."

I thought about it and it didn't make a bit of sense. I was Justa Williams, and my family, my two brothers and myself and our father, Howard, occupied a considerable ranch called the Half-Moon down along the Gulf of Mexico in Matagorda County, Texas. It was some of the best grazing land in the state and we had one of the best herds of purebred and crossbred cattle in that part of the country. In short we were pretty well-to-do.

But that didn't make us any the less ready to be stolen from, if indeed that was the case. The five-thousand acres Norris had been talking about had come to us through a trade our father had made some years before. We'd never made any use of it mainly because, as Ben had said, it was pretty worthless land, because it was a good two-hundred miles from our ranch headquarters. On a few occasions we'd bought cattle in Mexico and then used the acreage to hold small groups on while we made up a herd. But other than that, it lay mainly forgotten.

I frowned. "Norris, this doesn't make a damn bit of sense. Right after supper send a man into Blessing with a return wire for Jack asking him if he's certain. What the hell kind of squatting could anybody be doing on that land?"

Ben said, "Maybe they're raisin' watermelons." He laughed.

I said, "They could raise melons, but there damn sure wouldn't be no water in them."

Norris said, "Well, it bears looking into." He got up, throwing his napkin on the table. "I'll go write out that telegram."

I watched him go, dressed, as always, in his town clothes. Norris was the businessman in the family. He'd been sent down to the University at Austin and had got considerable learning about the ins and outs of banking and land deals and all the other parts of our business that didn't directly involve the ranch. At the age of twenty-nine I'd been the boss of the operation a good deal longer than I cared to think about. It had been thrust upon me by our father when I wasn't much more than twenty. He'd said he'd wanted me to take over while he was still strong enough to help me out of my mistakes and I reckoned that was partly true. But it had just seemed that after our mother had died the life had sort of gone out of him. He'd been one of the earliest settlers, taking up the land not long after Texas had become a republic in 1845. I figured all the years of fighting Indians and then Yankees and scalawags and carpetbaggers and cattle thieves had taken their toll on him. Then a few years back he'd been nicked in the lungs by a bullet that should never have been allowed to head his way and it had thrown an extra strain on his heart. He was pushing seventy and he still had plenty of head on his shoulders, but mostly all he did now was sit around in his rocking chair and stare out over the cattle and land business he'd built. Not to say that I didn't go to him for advice when the occasion demanded. I did, and mostly I took it.

Buttercup came in just then and sat down at the end of the table with a cup of coffee. He was near as old as Dad and almost completely worthless. But he'd been one of the first hands that Dad had hired and he'd been kept on even after he couldn't sit a horse anymore. The problem was he'd elected himself cook, and that was the sorriest day our family had ever seen. There were two Mexican women hired to cook for the twelve riders we kept full time, but Buttercup insisted on cooking for the family.

Mainly, I think, because he thought he was one of the family. A notion we could never completely dissuade him from.

So he sat there, about two days of stubble on his face, looking as scrawny as a pecked-out rooster, sweat running down his face, his apron a mess. He said, wiping his forearm across his forehead, "Boy, it shore be hot in there. You boys shore better be glad you ain't got no business takes you in that kitchen."

Ben said, in a loud mutter, "I wish you didn't either."

Ben, at twenty-five, was easily the best man with a horse or a gun that I had ever seen. His only drawback was that he was hotheaded and he tended to act first and think later. That ain't a real good combination for someone that could go on the prod as fast as Ben. When I had argued with Dad about taking over as boss, suggesting instead that Norris, with his education, was a much better choice, Dad had simply said, "Yes, in some ways. But he can't handle Ben. You can. You can handle Norris, too. But none of them can handle you."

Well, that hadn't been exactly true. If Dad had wished it I would have taken orders from Norris even though he was two years younger than me. But the logic in Dad's line of thinking had been that the Half-Moon and our cattle business was the lodestone of all our businesses and only I could run that. He had been right. In the past I'd imported purebred Whiteface and Hereford cattle from up North, bred them to our native Longhorns and produced cattle that would bring

177

twice as much at market as the horse-killing, all-bone, all-wild Longhorns. My neighbors had laughed at me at first, claiming those square little purebreds would never make it in our Texas heat. But they'd been wrong and, one by one, they'd followed the example of the Half-Moon.

Buttercup was setting up to take off on another one of his long-winded harrangues about how it had been in the "old days" so I quickly got up, excusing myself, and went into the big office we used for sitting around in as well as a place of business. Norris was at the desk composing his telegram so I poured myself out a whiskey and sat down. I didn't want to hear about any trouble over some worthless five-thousand acres of borderland. In fact I didn't want to hear about any troubles of any kind. I was just two weeks short of getting married, married to a lady I'd been courting off and on for five years, and I was mighty anxious that nothing come up to interfere with our plans. Her name was Nora Parker and her daddy owned and run the general mercantile in our nearest town, Blessing. I'd almost lost her once before to a Kansas City drummer. She'd finally gotten tired of waiting on me, waiting until the ranch didn't occupy all my time, and almost run off with a smooth-talking Kansas City drummer that called on her daddy in the harness trade. But she'd come to her senses in time and got off the train in Texarkana and returned home.

But even then it had been a close thing. I, along with my men and brothers and help from some of our neighbors, had been involved with stopping a huge herd of illegal cattle being driven up from Mexico from crossing our range and infecting our cattle with tick fever which could have wiped us all out. I tell you it had been a bloody business. We'd lost four good men and had to kill at least a half dozen on the other side. Fact of the business was I'd come about as close as I ever had to getting killed myself, and that was going some for the sort of rough-and-tumble life I'd led.

Nora had almost quit me over it, saying she just couldn't take the uncertainty. But in the end, she'd stuck by me. That had been the year before, 1896, and I'd convinced her that civilized law was coming to the country, but until it did, we that had been there before might have to take things into our own hands from time to time.

She'd seen that and had understood. I loved her and she loved me and that was enough to overcome any of the troubles we were still likely to encounter from day to day.

So I was giving Norris a pretty sour look as he finished his telegram and sent for a hired hand to ride it into Blessing, seven miles away. I said, "Norris, let's don't make a big fuss about this. That land ain't even crossed my mind in at least a couple of years. Likely we got a few Mexican families squatting down there and trying to scratch out a few acres of corn."

Norris gave me his businessman's look. He said, "It's our land, Justa. And if we allow anyone to squat on it for long enough or put up a fence they can lay claim. That's the law. My job is to see that we protect what we have, not give it away."

I sipped at my whiskey and studied Norris. In his town clothes he didn't look very impressive. He'd inherited more from our mother than from Dad so he was not as wide shouldered and slim-hipped as Ben and me. But I knew him to be a good, strong, dependable man in any kind of fight. Of course he wasn't that good with a gun, but then Ben and I weren't all that good with books like he was. But I said, just to jolly him a bit, "Norris, I do believe you are running to suet. I may have to put you out with Ben working the horse herd and work a little of that fat off you."

Naturally it got his goat. Norris had always envied Ben and me a little. I was just over six foot and weighed right around one-hundred and ninety. I had inherited my daddy's big hands and big shoulders. Ben was almost a copy of me except he was about a size smaller. Norris said, "I weigh the same as I have for the last five years. If it's any of your business."

I said, as if I was being serious, "Must be them sack suits you wear. What they do, pad them around the middle?"

He said, "Why don't you just go to hell."

After he'd stomped out of the room I got the bottle of whiskey and an extra glass and went down to Dad's room. It had been one of his bad days and he'd taken to bed right after lunch. Strictly speaking he wasn't supposed to have no whiskey, but I watered him down a shot every now and then and it didn't seem to do him no harm.

179

He was sitting up when I came in the room. I took a moment to fix him a little drink, using some water out of his pitcher, then handed him the glass and sat down in the easy chair by the bed. I told him what Norris had reported and asked what he thought.

He took a sip of his drink and shook his head. "Beats all I ever heard." he said. "I took that land in trade for a bad debt some fifteen, twenty years ago. I reckon I'd of been money ahead if I'd of hung on to the bad debt. That land won't even raise weeds, well as I remember, and Noah was in on the last rain that fell on the place."

We had considerable amounts of land spotted around the state as a result of this kind of trade or that. It was Norris's business to keep up with their management. I was just bringing this to Dad's attention more out of boredom and impatience for my wedding day to arrive than anything else.

I said, "Well, it's a mystery to me. How you feeling?"

He half smiled. "Old." Then he looked into his glass. "And I never liked watered whiskey. Pour me a dollop of the straight stuff in here."

I said, "Now, Howard. You know—"

He cut me off. "If I wanted somebody to argue with I'd send for Buttercup. Now do like I told you."

I did, but I felt guilty about it. He took the slug of whiskey down in one pull. Then he leaned his head back on the pillow and said, "Aaaaah. I don't give a damn what that horse doctor says, ain't nothing makes a man feel as good inside as a shot of the best."

I felt sorry for him laying there. He'd always led just the kind of life he wanted—going where he wanted, doing what he wanted, having what he set out to get. And now he was reduced to being a semi-invalid. But one thing that showed the strength that was still in him was that you *never* heard him complain. He said, "How's the cattle?"

I said, "They're doing all right, but I tell you we could do with a little of Noah's flood right now. All this heat and no rain is curing the grass off way ahead of time. If it doesn't let up we'll be feeding hay by late September, early October. And that will play hell on our supply. Could be we won't have enough to last through the winter. Norris thinks we ought to sell off five hundred head or so, but the market is doing poorly right now. I'd rather chance the weather than take a sure beating by selling off."

He sort of shrugged and closed his eyes. The whiskey was relaxing him. He said, "You're the boss."

"Yeah," I said. "Damn my luck."

I wandered out of the back of the house. Even though it was nearing seven o'clock of the evening it was still good and hot. Off in the distance, about a half a mile away, I could see the outline of the house I was building for Nora and myself. It was going to be a close thing to get it finished by our wedding day. Not having any riders to spare for the project, I'd imported a building contractor from Galveston, sixty miles away. He'd arrived with a half a dozen Mexican laborers and a few skilled masons and they'd set up a little tent city around the place. The contractor had gone back to Galveston to fetch more materials, leaving his Mexicans behind. I walked along idly, hoping he wouldn't forget that the job wasn't done. He had some of my money, but not near what he'd get when he finished the job.

Just then Ray Hays came hurrying across the back lot toward me. Ray was kind of a special case for me. The only problem with that was that he knew it and wasn't a bit above taking advantage of the situation. Once, a few years past, he'd saved my life by going against an evil man that he was working for at the time, an evil man who meant to have my life. In gratitude I'd given Ray a good job at the Half-Moon, letting him work directly under Ben, who was responsible for the horse herd. He was a good, steady man and a good man with a gun. He was also fair company. When he wasn't talking.

He came churning up to me, mopping his brow. He said, "Lordy, boss, it is—"

I said, "Hays, if you say it's hot I'm going to knock you down."

He gave me a look that was a mixture of astonishment and hurt. He said, "Why, whatever for?"

I said, "*Everybody* knows it's hot. Does every son of a bitch you run into have to make mention of the fact?"

His brow furrowed. "Well, I never thought of it that way. I 'spect you are right. Goin' down to look at yore house?"

I shook my head. "No. It makes me nervous to see how far they've got to go. I can't see any way it'll be ready on time."

He said, "Miss Nora ain't gonna like that."

I gave him a look. "I guess you felt forced to say that."

He looked down. "Well, maybe she won't mind."

I said, grimly, "The hell she won't. She'll think I did it a-purpose."

"Aw, she wouldn't."

"Naturally you know so much about it, Hays. Why don't you tell me a few other things about her."

"I was jest tryin' to lift yore spirits, boss."

I said, "You keep trying to lift my spirits and I'll put you on the haying crew."

He looked horrified. No real cowhand wanted any work he couldn't do from the back of his horse. Haying was a hot, hard, sweaty job done either afoot or from a wagon seat. We generally brought in contract Mexican labor to handle ours. But I'd been known in the past to discipline a cowhand by giving him a few days on the hay gang. Hays said, "Boss, now I never meant nothin'. I swear. You know me, my mouth gets to runnin' sometimes. I swear I'm gonna watch it."

I smiled. Hays always made me smile. He was so easily buffaloed. He had it soft at the Half-Moon and he knew it and didn't want to take any chances on losing a good thing.

I lit up a cigarillo and watched dusk settle in over the coastal plains. It wasn't but three miles to Matagorda Bay and it was quiet enough I felt like I could almost hear the waves breaking on the shore. Somewhere in the distance a mama cow bawled for her calf. The spring crop were near about weaned by now, but there were still a few mamas that wouldn't cut the apron strings. I stood there reflecting on how peaceful things had been of late. It suited me just fine. All I wanted was to get my house finished, marry Nora and never handle another gun so long as I lived.

The peace and quiet were short-lived. Within twenty-four hours we'd had a return telegram from Jack Cole. It said:

YOUR LAND OCCUPIED BY TEN TO TWELVE MEN STOP
CAN'T BE SURE WHAT THEY'RE DOING BECAUSE

THEY RUN STRANGERS OFF STOP APPEAR TO HAVE A
GOOD MANY CATTLE GATHERED STOP APPEAR TO BE
FENCING STOP ALL I KNOW STOP

I read the telegram twice and then I said, "Why this is crazy
as hell! That land wouldn't support fifty head of cattle."

We were all gathered in the big office. Even Dad was there,
sitting in his rocking chair. I looked up at him. "What do you
make of this, Howard?"

He shook his big, old head of white hair. "Beats the hell out
of me, Justa. I can't figure it."

Ben said, "Well, I don't see where it has to be figured. I'll
take five men and go down there and run them off. I don't care
what they're doing. They ain't got no business on our land."

I said, "Take it easy, Ben. Aside from the fact you don't
need to be getting into any more fights this year, I can't spare
you or five men. The way this grass is drying up we've got
to keep drifting those cattle."

Norris said, "No, Ben is right. We can't have such affairs
going on with our property. But we'll handle it within the law.
I'll simply take the train down there, hire a good lawyer and
have the matter settled by the sheriff. Shouldn't take but a few
days."

Well, there wasn't much I could say to that. We couldn't
very well let people take advantage of us, but I still hated to
be without Norris's services even for a few days. On matters
other than the ranch he was the expert, and it didn't seem like
there was a day went by that some financial question didn't
come up that only he could answer. I said, "Are you sure you
can spare yourself for a few days?"

He thought for a moment and then nodded. "I don't see why
not. I've just moved most of our available cash into short-term
municipal bonds in Galveston. The market is looking all right
and everything appears fine at the bank. I can't think of anything that might come up."

I said, "All right. But you just keep this in mind. You
are not a gun hand. You are not a fighter. I do not want
you going anywhere near those people, whoever they are.
You do it legal and let the sheriff handle the eviction. Is that
understood?"

He kind of swelled up, resenting the implication that he couldn't handle himself. The biggest trouble I'd had through the years when trouble had come up had been keeping Norris out of it. Why he couldn't just be content to be a wagon load of brains was more than I could understand. He said, "Didn't you just hear me say I intended to go through a lawyer and the sheriff? Didn't I just say that?"

I said, "I wanted to be sure you heard yourself."

He said, "Nothing wrong with my hearing. Nor my approach to this matter. You seem to constantly be taken with the idea that I'm always looking for a fight. I think you've got the wrong brother. I use logic."

"Yeah?" I said. "You remember when that guy kicked you in the balls when they were holding guns on us? And then we chased them twenty miles and finally caught them?"

He looked away. "That has nothing to do with this."

"Yeah?" I said, enjoying myself. "And here's this guy, shot all to hell. And what was it you insisted on doing?"

Ben laughed, but Norris wouldn't say anything.

I said, "Didn't you insist on us standing him up so you could kick him in the balls? Didn't you?"

He sort of growled, "Oh, go to hell."

I said, "I just want to know where the logic was in that."

He said, "Right is right. I was simply paying him back in kind. It was the only thing his kind could understand."

I said, "That's my point. You just don't go down there and go to paying back a bunch of rough hombres in kind. Or any other currency for that matter."

That made him look over at Dad. He said, "Dad, will you make him quit treating me like I was ten years old? He does it on purpose."

But he'd appealed to the wrong man. Dad just threw his hands in the air and said, "Don't come to me with your troubles. I'm just a boarder around here. You get your orders from Justa. You know that."

Of course he didn't like that. Norris had always been a strong hand for the right and wrong of a matter. In fact, he may have been one of the most stubborn men I'd ever met. But he didn't say anything, just gave me a look and muttered something about hoping a mess came up at the bank while he was gone and then see how much boss I was.

But he didn't mean nothing by it. Like most families, we fought amongst ourselves and, like most families, God help the outsider who tried to interfere with one of us.

A special offer for people who enjoy reading the best Westerns published today. If you enjoyed this book, subscribe now and get...

TWO FREE

A $5.90 VALUE—NO OBLIGATION

If you enjoyed this book and would like to read more of the very best Westerns being published today, you'll want to subscribe to True Value's Western Home Subscription Service. If you enjoyed the book you just read and want more of the most exciting, adventurous, action packed Westerns, subscribe now.

Each month the editors of True Value will select the 6 very best Westerns from America's leading publishers for special readers like you. You'll be able to preview these new titles as soon as they are published, FREE for ten days with no obligation.

TWO FREE BOOKS

When you subscribe, we'll send you your first month's shipment of the newest and best 6 Westerns for you to preview. With your first shipment, two of these books will be yours as our introductory gift to you absolutely FREE, regardless of what you decide to do. If you like them, as much as we think you will, keep all six books but pay for just 4 at the low subscriber rate of just $2.45 each. If you decide to return them, keep 2 of the titles as our gift. No obligation.

Special Subscriber Savings

When you become a True Value subscriber you'll save money several ways. First, all regular monthly selections will be billed at the low subscriber price of just $2.45 each. That's

WESTERNS!

at least a savings of $3.00 each month below the publishers price. Second, there is never any shipping, handling or other hidden charges—Free home delivery. What's more there is no minimum number of books you must buy, you may return any selection for full credit and you can cancel your subscription at any time. A TRUE VALUE!

Mail the coupon below

To start your subscription and receive 2 FREE WESTERNS, fill out the coupon below and mail it today. We'll send your first shipment which includes 2 FREE BOOKS as soon as we receive it.

Mail To: **10649**
True Value Home Subscription Services, Inc.
P.O. Box 5235
120 Brighton Road
Clifton, New Jersey 07015-5235

YES! I want to start receiving the very best Westerns being published today. Send me my first shipment of 6 Westerns for me to preview FREE for 10 days. If I decide to keep them, I'll pay for just 4 of the books at the low subscriber price of $2.45 each; a total of $9.80 (a $17.70 value). Then each month I'll receive the 6 newest and best Westerns to preview Free for 10 days. If I'm not satisfied I may return them within 10 days and owe nothing. Otherwise I'll be billed at the special low subscriber rate of $2.45 each; a total of $14.70 (at least a $17.70 value) and save $3.00 off the publishers price. There are never any shipping, handling or other hidden charges. I understand I am under no obligation to purchase any number of books and I can cancel my subscription at any time, no questions asked. In any case the 2 FREE books are mine to keep.

Name _____

Address _____ Apt. # _____

City _____ State _____ Zip _____

Telephone # _____

Signature _____
(if under 18 parent or guardian must sign)
Terms and prices subject to change.
Orders subject to acceptance by True Value Home Subscription Services, Inc.

LONGARM

Explore the exciting Old West with
one of the men who made it wild!

___LONGARM AND THE VIGILANTES #140   0-515-10385-3/$2.95
___LONGARM IN THE OSAGE STRIP #141   0-515-10401-9/$2.95
___LONGARM AND THE LOST MINE #142   0-515-10426-4/$2.95
___LONGARM AND THE LONGLEY   0-515-10445-0/$2.95
   LEGEND #143
___LONGARM AND THE DEAD MAN'S   0-515-10472-8/$2.95
   BADGE #144
___LONGARM AND THE KILLER'S   0-515-10494-9/$2.95
   SHADOW #145
___LONGARM AND THE MONTANA   0-515-10512-0/$2.95
   MASSACRE #146
___LONGARM IN THE MEXICAN   0-515-10526-0/$2.95
   BADLANDS #147
___LONGARM AND THE BOUNTY HUNTRESS   0-515-10547-3/$2.95
   #148
___LONGARM AND THE DENVER   0-515-10570-8/$2.95
   BUST-OUT #149
___LONGARM AND THE SKULL CANYON   0-515-10597-X/$2.95
   GANG #150
___LONGARM AND THE RAILROAD TO HELL   0-515-10613-5/$3.50
   #151
___LONGARM AND THE LONE STAR CAPTIVE   0-515-10646-1/$4.50
   (Giant novel)
___LONGARM AND THE RIVER OF DEATH #152   0-515-10649-6/$3.50